The Eyes of the Beholder

Book 1

by Roman Valentine

DORRANCE
PUBLISHING CO
EST. 1920
PITTSBURGH, PENNSYLVANIA 15238

Dorrance Publishing Co
585 Alpha Drive
Suite 103
Pittsburgh, PA 15238
Visit our website at *www.dorrancebookstore.com*

ISBN: 978-1-6386-7096-4
eISBN: 978-1-6386-7916-5

C Table of Contents

8:00 AM:
The Gimura Mountain Hideout

It was that time again; the time Imara dreaded the most as she shined her blade and joined the rest of her family. Imara, her mother, and her siblings had to line up in order, in front of her father for headcount. Despite not wanting to do it, she was still in line at 8:00 AM, as expected.

The moment Imara's father stepped into the main room was the moment all went silent and everyone in the family stiffened up for headcount. The patriarch of the family glared for a moment, bringing his double-edged trident to bear as he surveyed his family.

"Good morning, Raj," the wife greeted with a smile. The man simply narrowed his eyes.

"Who?" It was one very stiff word, but she got the point. Today was one of those days.

"Good morning, Master Maharajan." To that, the obstreperous father acknowledged his wife's greetings.

"And a very good morning to you too, Penelope," he said, noticing her weapon wasn't unsheathed and at display. "You're not

1

battle ready," he said simply. To that, Penelope simply held up her assault rifle.

"Better," he said, as the man walked in front of his oldest child.

"Good morning, Master Maharajan." The twenty-two-year-old man sounded off, his voice strong and masculine as he did. Raj simply smiled.

"Good morning to you too, Adam." Raj nodded in pride at the sight of his son's sword, not even caring that it wasn't cleaned.

He moved on to his second child, an intellectually inclined nineteen-year-old who at six foot three stood five full inches taller than his father and older brother. He could see over his father's head, but was not allowed to look down as he sounded off in his rather soft tenor voice. "Good morning, Master Maharajan." His sword was quite a bit thinner and more needle-like than the broadsword his older brother Adam wielded, which just reinforced the difference in musculature between the two.

"Good morning, Jericho."

Imara was third, or would have been third, had the father not immediately passed over her and stopped in front of his third son and youngest child. Even Penelope seemed shocked at this, but the fourth child sounded off, his voice clearly indicating that he was no older than thirteen. "Good morning, Master Maharajan!" he said with utmost enthusiasm. The strict father's facade cracked for just a moment to flicker a smile at his youngest son. His platinum-lined spear was impeccably cleaned and seemed to glow even in the dark hideout, unlike the weapons of his two older brothers. It might have even been as clean as Imara's, if only Raj would acknowledge it.

"And good morning to you, Hassan."

Raj walked past Imara once again, pointedly trying to ignore the sole, rather unique-looking daughter in his household. Penelope was dumbfounded, but knew better than to challenge her husband when he was in the best of moods, let alone on a morning like this. His expression turning stone cold before he spoke more than sealed it.

"Our scout has returned. As usual, you . . ." he pointed his trident at his daughter, "prove yet again just how much you shame our family name!" Raj's wrath was sudden, and terrifying. His mood was assuaged just a bit as she hid her rather displeasing looking face in fear; as if to spite him further, Imara's face was a face that he didn't like seeing at all. He wondered why she alone was born so ugly, and how she could be born at all from a beautiful mother like Penelope.

"Raj, she—" Penelope attempted, before Raj held up his hand to silence her as he returned to his now trembling daughter.

"You allowed your ugly face to be seen by some kids near the village! Why? Well?! I asked you a question!" he ranted, and Imara stammered out her answer.

"Th-they needed help, and-and-and there weren't any . . . any adults around and . . ." Raj's expression only twisted further as he heard Imara's words.

"Help? You should have let those bastards be eaten by those lions. Now, because of your weakness, they will suffer!" Even the sons had started to become uncomfortable with Raj's implications, but not one of them dared voice it. Not now.

Raj turned to the entrance of the hideout. "Move out! Adam, Jericho, Hassan! Lead your units as you see fit! Penelope . . ." Raj faltered for just a moment when he looked at Imara, and especially at the serrated blade she carried. It took him a moment to steel himself against the fact that the offending, ugly daughter wielded that offending scimitar. "You and her make yourselves as useful as you can. But don't hinder us. Understood?" Raj glared at Imara as he said this.

The daughter squeaked out an affirmative, as Penelope stepped between them. "We understand Raj." She said as coolly and calmly as she could. Raj nodded. He turned to the men gathered outside of the main cave, all fifty of them gathered and awaiting orders as Adam, Hassan, and Jericho appeared before them. Raj made his appearance at that moment.

"We move! Gimura Force, set out!" he ordered, as he led his wife and sons to the force's van-like vehicle. Pointedly, Imara was not allowed to ride with the rest of her family, being forced to ride with the subordinates with the rest of the land fleet.

She was just happy to be allowed to join her family at all, really.

9:30 AM:
Janihar Village,
Southern River Area

Raj laughed at just how easy this was; the civilians of this small Elven township scattered and scampered about as his bandit force tore through their daily routines and began to plunder everything of value. Just like all the villages before the Gimura Force visited, the civilians would all be picked off, one by one, by each of the fifty men under his employ. His three sons, as usual, led their small band as efficiently as any military unit he had ever seen or encountered. The village militia, despite previous warning, just could not prepare for the elite outlaw unit that he himself personally trained.

And all done using my teachings, Raj thought as he held up his hand to freeze some bullets in their tracks. Only a handful of the militiamen could react in time to avoid having their fire returned to them with twice the force, but Raj still managed to hit all but six of his twenty targets. As they hit the floor and Raj savored his work, he didn't see that one of the six survivors had managed to dodge out of his sight. Raj heard him, however, and he swung his trident as he turned. This forced the militiaman to duck and attempt a sweep. Raj perhaps knew that was coming and simply jumped back. Now with positions reset, the militiaman drew his pistol and attempted to shoot the leader of the Gimura Force dead. Raj found himself using his defensive aura yet again to shield himself from the bullets, but before he could turn the bullets back at his adversary, the volunteer had brought his retractable spear to its full length and attempted to run Raj through. Raj just barely dodged, as he wielded his double-edged trident like the master staff-fighter he was.

Unfortunately, the militiaman in front of him was also a quite proficient staff-fighter, and that translated to defensive ability as he blocked every spin and strike from the trident. He made an attempt at a slash, causing Raj to jump back. He summoned up his inner chi and directed it into the strongest blast he could muster. Unfortunately, the militiaman was ready and countered with a well-placed throwing knife. Although the blast managed to stagger the projectile blade's course, it wasn't a total redirection.

The cold steel slid right into Raj's thigh as if the flesh was made of hot butter. An agonizing moment of sheer pain preceded Raj's bloodcurdling scream.

"I got him? I just got the bandit leader!" The volunteer celebrated as Raj went down to one knee in agony. His focus lost, Raj couldn't summon up any magic, not any that would save him.

However, a miracle DID in fact happen for the leader of the Gimura Force. In the form of the last face he wanted to see. Before the volunteer civilian fighter could finish Raj off with his spear, Imara seized the opportunity to slice through the militiaman. Her cut was clean, for the man's head was immediately liberated from his body and it fell into the nearby river. He likely didn't even feel life end at that moment. "Dad, are you oka—"

If Imara was expecting gratitude from Raj, she was in for a rude awakening. "You stupid, ugly, failure! Why are you worried about me, when you should be helping your mother take as much as you can from the damned treasury?!" Raj snapped, his face cringing from the excruciating pain that jolted through his leg as he stood. Against her better judgment, Imara approached, her offhand alighting with an alternating blue and green aura. Raj knew that to be the Healer's Hand.

"You're hurt, Dad. Let me just . . ." she attempted, but Raj was having none of it.

"I told you to go confiscate everything in the treasury! I will continue to fight!" he barked out. Before he could say anything further, however, a voice and face he did want to see and hear made itself known.

"Raj? Raj are you okay?" It was Penelope, her assault rifle carried over her shoulder. "I sent Imara here to tell you that she and I cleared out the treasury. And Imara set fire to the remaining armories and granary depots on her way here. With that, the official in charge of this village should be surrendering any moment now." Raj's smile disappeared, but unlike the twisted visage of rage he held with Imara, this expression was one of understanding and reasoning.

"Penelope, we can't show these spoiled citizens any mercy. Not after how the emperor's court treated me. Treated this family . . ." The three of them saw more militiamen approaching.

"You need to get back to the hideout. The battle is won, anyway. Imara and I will take it from here." she said. Raj scoffed.

"Penelope, make sure she doesn't hold you back." Raj scorned, as he limped away to the direction of the land fleet. Imara put her father's harsh words out of her head as she and Penelope began to steel themselves for the coming battle.

"Don't worry about him, Imara. Your father . . . is dealing with a lot." For what it was worth, that wasn't a lie. But even Penelope had to know how flat and flimsy that excuse truly was. In any case, now was not the time to think about that.

Imara conjured up some more ammo for her mother; the armor piercing, anti-magic rounds were perhaps unneeded for this situation but both mother and daughter could never be too careful. As soon as the militiamen came within the assault rifle's range, Imara held out her scimitar in a defensive stance and closed her eyes, successfully summoning Hajitar's Shield to protect herself and her mother from any magic blasts, bullets, or other projectiles. Fortunately for the mother-daughter duo, Hajitar's Shield wasn't two-way; Penelope could still mow down her opponents just as easily as if the mystical barrier had not been there at all.

Penelope ran out of ammo again, at the same time that Imara's arms got tired as she felt the constant pressure of the bullets pounding on the summoned energy shield. Just as soon as she dropped the shield was the moment the remaining ten out of eighty militiamen were able to get a good look at Imara's weapon of choice.

"A Troll Scimitar?! The enemy possesses a Troll Scimitar!" one of them yelled in panic.

"Those fools! They're letting a mere child wield it?!" another screamed out in panic.

"Don't panic! The reports were true, that's all. We need to retreat and regroup with our Village Chief," one of the calmer volunteers said, but noticeably even he was startled by what he witnessed.

Penelope and Imara looked at one another as each and every single remaining foe retreated, before seizing the opportunity to also make their escape.

Once they were far enough away, the mother and daughter duo laughed hysterically at the survivor's reactions.

11:00 AM:
Gimura Force Hideout
Convergence Room

All fifty members of the Gimura Force had survived the raid; except for being scuffed or some minor cuts everyone was alive, standing and accounted for. All five members of Raj's household had returned to him alive, and as he limped into the main room of the hideout to do a survey of what they looted, his injury was nagging him. But for what it was worth he allowed it to be bandaged by one of the medics in the Force. The Healer's Hand would be applied later, though Imara was tempted to volunteer for the job once again. However, she knew better than to broach the subject, especially now as he limped before his family.

As usual, first he stood before Penelope. "I have returned, Master Maharajan!" she said, though there was clearly an edge of exasperation to the wife's voice. She did not hold her weapon where he could see it, but right now Raj didn't care as he nodded and moved on to Adam.

"I have returned, Master Maharajan!" Once again, the eldest son had sounded off as powerfully as he was built, and just like Penelope it was noticed that his weapon wasn't brought to bear either. Raj moved on, just as he did with Penelope.

Imara dreaded what she knew was coming, but for now Raj stopped in front of his leaner second son. "I have returned, Master Maharajan!" The other fifty members of the Gimura Force knew better than to laugh at just how much less manly Jericho sounded compared to his older, shorter brother, but Raj's glare at them told them that he knew exactly what they were thinking. Once again, Jericho's longsword was allowed to remain lazily at his side.

Imara was expecting Raj to bypass her again, but this time, he stopped. He did not look at his only daughter. That just could not mean anything good. "First, you endanger my life on the battlefield, then you disobey direct orders, and NOW you don't even have the courtesy to bring your weapon to bear during lineup!" Penelope, Adam, Jericho, and Hassan now turned to the patriarch in shock.

Imara shook in fear, as the rest of the Force seemed to become tense at Raj's attitude. "What do you have to say for yourself, you ugly failure!?" Imara's eyes filled with tears, but unfortunately this meant she failed to answer her father when he addressed her. And that failure was going to cost her. Almost faster than anyone could see, the back of Raj's fist collided with Imara's temple, knocking her clear off her feet. Her battle armor rattled as she hit the floor.

"Imara!" Penelope screamed in concern. Before Raj could silence any further dissent, he found the tip of a platinum spear being pointed at his jugular. Hassan had gotten between him and the fallen Gimura daughter.

"Back off! She gets the point!" The teenaged warrior commanded. The Gimura Force all seemed to be ready to move, but Raj paid them no heed. For a moment he hesitated, before he took a step back. A proud smile spread across his face.

"Standing up for even the ugliest failure among us. You're going to make a wonderful prince once I seize the crown, Hassan." His face turned serious as he looked to his two older sons. "And that is why Hassan will be joining you two in your next scouting assignment." Raj then looked to the recovering daughter, who was being assisted by Penelope and a few of the other male members of the Force. Hassan pointedly did not move out of the way, though he did in fact lower his spear when his father had backed off.

"Don't let her disappoint me again."

7:00 AM
the Next Morning

Imara felt almost happy; her parents weren't awake just yet, and the sun was just now peeking over the horizon. Imara did not put on her battle armor; this was a scouting mission and therefore discretion was of the utmost importance. In her worn gray skirt, black t-shirt, and tan boots, she looked pretty much like any other peasant girl who'd be out and about with her brothers. "In covert missions, my ugly face comes in handy, doesn't it?" She sarcastically jibed to no one in particular, repeating her father's favorite insult toward her aloud. "Ugly failure, eh?"

Even in the peasant clothes that she wore to be discrete, Imara knew she cut an impressive figure in the mirror before her. Sure, she had been a homely baby and only slightly prettier little child, but since hitting puberty she'd lost most of her baby fat. Standing in the mirror was a curvy five foot seven, 160 pound, seventeen-year-old with olive skin and long, luscious black hair. Imara showed no cleavage, but her ample bosom was still very clearly present under her t-shirt, and she was certainly proud of her endowment. However, she was twice as proud of her curvy hips and back side and then three times as proud of her shapely legs, which the peasant skirt showed off really well. She didn't wear the shorts her mother picked out; the skirt hid her curvy backside well. And that really was the point in this mission of blending in.

She looked at her offending face. The long, pointed nose and sharp ears that displayed her Elven heritage, and the wide gremlin-like eyes really were off-putting. Imara forced herself to smile in the mirror, for her full, pillowy lips that framed her perfect teeth was her face's only saving grace. But so long as she wasn't in her battle armor, there would never be a reason to look at the face that angered her father so much.

As soon as she stepped outside, there were her brothers waiting for her. When Raj wasn't around, there was almost an air of joviality and camaraderie among the Gimura family. Like their sister, the three Gimura brothers were dressed as modestly and commonly as possible. They looked pretty much like any regular citizen outside of their Gimura Force battle armor. Imara could also notice that a fourth, unrelated male was also present, dressed as commonly as the rest of them.

"Ron? You're letting Ron join us?" Ron chuckled.

"More like I'm tagging along whether they want me to or not, but yes." Imara's face brightened even further when her closest friend confirmed this and everyone laughed. In all honesty, Ronmaru "Ron" Jotomatu was better defined as a family friend of the Gimura family, but for Imara he was about the only young male outside of her family that she interacted with on a regular basis in a non-combat or platonic situation.

"So, where're we goin' again?" Ron asked as they all entered the van, and Imara checked her map.

"According to this map, we're crossing the border and scouting the city of Kidojoa." Jericho almost didn't want to start the ignition of the van when he heard that.

"Wait, time out. Didn't the reports say that the Prince of the Masai Kingdom is visiting there soon?"

Jericho's cautious nature reared its head here, to which Adam scoffed, "Yeah? That's kind of dad's plan here." Jericho turned on the ignition.

"It's not a good one." The strategic brother said as they drove out of the hideout. As usual, Imara sat in the passenger seat when Raj wasn't around; she cherished moments like this when she was allowed to be included with her family.

"Raj has never had the best plans, now has he?" Ron pointed out, and Imara silently concurred. It was Adam who'd say it, however.

"No, but he's always had a semblance of an idea when it comes to leading the Gimura Force in the past. Eight years, and we've only had to replace ten members of the Force. Eight years, and not one raid has turned up empty handed. Nor has the Empress's forces caught up to us," Adam explained. Jericho did not take his eyes off the road as he responded.

"The Empress passed him over in favor of our uncle for a reason, though." Imara became tense, remembering how often her father berated her due to her magical talent. Adam hesitated for a moment, before he feebly gave his answer.

"He at least can summon a protective aura and redirect bullets using his physical energy alone, so there's that." Even Adam probably knew exactly why that wasn't special, but Ron was going to tell him anyway.

"Ha! That's it? We're going to be passing by gyms full of meatheads too stubborn to quit who can do that. Matter of fact, Penelope can summon a protective aura around herself if she's mad, scared, or desperate enough." Ron laughed at just how inept at magic Raj truly was, despite having attended sorcery school twice.

It wasn't like Raj's scions didn't agree. "Really, he should be more proud of me than he is." Imara finally felt it safe to speak up. And Adam and Hassan rewarded it by agreeing with her.

"Yeah, he should be. You've got some serious talent, sis. The weapon you wield each and every day in battle is proof enough of that." Adam's words made the Gimura sister beam with silent pride, but that her brothers could recognize her talent just highlighted the fact that Raj could not. Ron's words just spelled it out further.

"You know, if Raj is really so concerned about it, the answer to his problems is riding shotgun in this van. Matter of fact, that's true of pretty much every problem Raj founded this Force to solve." Ron's words were absolutely correct, but not one of the four Gimura siblings wanted to admit it. Imara, in fact, knew just how right Ron's words were, and just how many arguments Raj could make those words apply to. However, good luck getting the Gimura patriarch to listen to those words.

"But he's not!" Hassan said, once again taking the words out of anyone else's mouth. "Between Adam's strength and Jerry's strategies, Dad has everything he needs to lead a coup against the Empress if he wanted. He lets Imara share her talent in sorcery with the rest of the men, and there's nothing we can't do." Hassan said, and the older people in the van concurred, if silently.

"Hassan, we all know why he won't, though." Imara said, her dejected tone summarizing the mood that Raj could bring about to those closest to him, without the man himself even being present.

They rode in silence the rest of the way there, but it was only twenty minutes before they finally crossed the border.

They were greeted by a border patrolman, making Jericho happy that he chose the family van for this mission as opposed to using one of the armored vehicles of the land fleet. He honestly couldn't believe he made that mistake before. "Alright, everyone, be cool." Adam said, though he really didn't have to give that order. In any case, the patrolman made it to the van.

"Hmm . . ." he said as he looked into the van. Everyone did their best to play it cool, and for what it was worth they certainly looked like college and high school kids on a road trip right now. "You kids seem familiar," he said, as he held up a piece of paper. They all dreaded that it was a wanted poster, but the confirmation along with the relief of any suspicion that may have been cast upon them came quickly.

"Be careful kids. You may be elves, but this man here is well known as a bandit and an enemy to the public. The emperor of this land welcomes visitors from even the Elven Territories, but he also wants all visitors to understand the danger they are in visiting even these parts." The patrolman never suspected that these were the offspring of former General Maharajan Gimura, nor did they suspect that they were the niece and nephews of Imperial Counselor Tajaharu Gimura. He also didn't seem to know that Ronmaru was the son of Maharajan's accomplice in the attempted coup. However, the patrolman wasn't done just yet.

"But so long as you stay near Kidojoa for the time being, you kids will be safe. Not even the Gimura Force or the Mansa Army would be so bold as to attack while the Crown Prince and his royal vanguard are there. If anything . . ." The man had been making his way over to the passenger side of the van as he spoke, appearing to do a scan of the vehicle until it was noticed that he stopped in front of Imara.

"The greatest threat in the land right now is sitting right here." Imara didn't know whether the flirtatious tone this patrolman took was a good sign or a bad sign. "It's my job to ensure that the royal family knows when a threat to the Crown Prince's virtue and clarity of mind has entered their lands," he said, causing Imara's face to involuntarily redden at the patrolman's veiled flirtations. Her brothers and Ronmaru crinkled their noses at how bold and blatant this man was, but they hadn't heard anything yet.

"For security reasons and to ensure the Crown Prince's clarity of mind as he prepares for his ascension, I might need to search that skirt of yours for any potential tools of distraction you may use on him." Imara's face softened at this; lecherous though this man was, she didn't quite know what to make of his compliments. Or just compliments concerning her appearance in general. Before anyone could say anything, the patrolman backed away from the van. "Have fun kids. Especially you, sugar lips." With that, the patrolman granted them permission to pass. As the van picked up speed, the flirty border guard winked at Imara one last time.

And Raj thinks she's unattractive . . . Ron thought.

7:00 PM that Evening:
Gimura Force Hideout

It was fun while it lasted; the van ride home was both the most fun and the most dreaded ride home in a long time. Their assignment completed by 4:00 in the afternoon, the young scouts knew it was time to report back. They spent one hour training in the outskirts of the city; Imara decided now was as good a time as any to share a little more of her knowledge and talent with her brothers while she could. Of course, her brothers would never tell their father of what they were introduced to, and Ron especially was not going to share any of what they discussed on the van ride to or from Kidojoa.

Raj and Penelope were waiting for them. As soon as the van parked in the carport, all within the vehicle were to line up in order for the report. Imara's mood shot, she almost soullessly went through the motions. They did not have their weapons, so there was no need to hold it at the ready. Some of the Gimura Force was also present during this report; Imara could almost feel most of their eyes on her as they beheld the Gimura daughter in something else besides her training GI or her battle armor. As a matter of fact, Imara couldn't remember the last time she had seen any of them outside of training or combat; her father need only to go through that ordeal once to make sure she didn't get too close to the men again.

"I've returned, Dad." Adam said in a lackadaisical tone, and it was really noticed just how much emphasis he put on his lazy, muttering greeting. It was doubly noticeable when Raj didn't so much as flinch at the very obvious breach of protocol that Adam committed by saying "Dad" instead of referring to him the way a subordinate would address a County Chief. Raj moved on to his second son.

"I have returned, Dad." Raj nodded at his taller son, also pointedly not caring at all that Jericho clearly did not address the former County Chief correctly. Once again, Imara is passed over, and once again she can't help but feel the lack of regard and respect her father had for her. However, she was determined to keep her sinking mood from sinking any further. Not until it had to, so to speak.

"I'm back, Dad." Hassan did not even say "I have returned," and Raj did not so much as blink when he heard his son greet him this way during a report. Imara almost audibly sighed in relief when Raj didn't come back to her, as he stopped before Ron. He did not wait for the younger man to greet him.

"The map. And a report of anything pertinent to this city's defenses," Raj ordered, and Imara produced the map that they drew up.

"She drew up the map?! You entrusted this failure to make my battle plans?" Raj snapped. Ron narrowed his eyes; he was as tall as Jericho, and about as powerfully built as Adam. Anyone else might have been intimidated, but Raj simply continued, "Did. She. Draw. The. Map?!" Raj seethed out. Adam and Jericho both stepped forward.

"She did. And we couldn't have gotten a map as detailed or accurate if not for the Sight of Oracles." Raj's arms tensed at the mention of one of those damned sorcerous techniques that had been the bane of his life. He snatched the map away from Imara. And at seeing the rough way he handled it, Adam spoke up.

"Hey! Be careful with that! Imara, Jericho, and I worked very hard on drawing that up! The least you can do is not tear it up before you even see it!" Adam said, finally standing up for his sister in the face of their father's attitude toward her.

"Are you going to side with the one who shames our family name, son?!" he threatened, now getting in his oldest son's face.

"What if I am?" Adam coldly said, throwing the challenge. The other members of the Force simply turned their heads, not wanting to see what Raj's reaction was going to be.

"According to the border patrol and pretty much every billboard and news station broadcast, the Crown Prince of the Masai Kingdom will be visiting in about three days." Ron said, starting with the biggest piece of information first and hoping to diffuse the situation. For what it was worth, he succeeded in de-escalating the situation. But the new look in Raj's eye as he heard confirmation sent chills down the younger, taller man's spine. Ron almost saw the words forming in Raj's mouth before he spoke to them.

"Perfect. Yes . . . YES! Perfect! Crown Prince Vituo is going to be mine! When news of his death reaches the Empress . . . Oh, she'll practically fall right out of her dress! She will regret the day she ever passed me over for promotion! And she will have no choice but to hand her kingdom over to me once I bring Vituo down!" Raj was practically slavering over the prospect of defeating the Elven Territories erstwhile enemy and ending the war in their favor. More than anything, he was also slavering over the fame that bringing down the Crown Prince of the strongest of the Kingdoms of Paradise would theoretically earn him.

Imara shifted uncomfortably, but Ron was more vocal, "Master Maharajan, with all due respect—"

Raj interjected, "You have a problem with the plan, boy?" Ron was a man of twenty-one, and hearing someone besides his father calling him a boy just irked him, superior rank or not. Before Ron could speak, however, the only man who had his implicit permission to refer to him as such spoke up.

"Raj, I want you to think about this." Raj turned, facing the one who spoke. And it was indeed Ron's father; more importantly, it was Raj's closest friend who had stuck with him through thick and thin. Even during the days before Raj founded the Gimura Force.

"Atto, what's there to think about? We form a plan, and then we catch our hostage. I've not led this Force astray in the past, and I won't start three days from now, when the prince is apprehended." He turned to his wife and then the other subordinates gathered. "Tell everyone to make the proper preparations. Three days from now, we move!"

Raj had dismissed everyone, clearly indicating he was in no mood for further discussion. Imara caught her father's glare, however, invoking an involuntary shudder from the disfavored daughter.

11:00 AM
the Next Morning

Raj smiled as he watched Atto and Ron lead the rest of the Force in their exercises. From battle formations, to drills, to sparring tournaments, the Gimura Force was perhaps as well trained as any true military unit in the Elven Territories. Raj felt pride swell up in his mind, but it was quickly dissipated by his wife's words.

"Raj, please . . . Just think about this. The plan you formed is . . ." Raj didn't turn to look at his wife.

"Is what?" he said lowly. Penelope was not about to be deterred, however.

"The city we are attacking will contain the Crown Prince of the Kingdom of Paradise. Even before we consider the power of a mastered Changeling, we also have to consider that he could have as many as two hundred of his elite bodyguards accompanying him. If that isn't bad enough, there's a good chance one or more of the subordinate Masai Five could be present with him as well. We won't just be up against a militia or even a small unit of troops. We can't attack this city as we normally do. Vituo won't be taken so easily."

Raj seemed to think for just a moment, before he responded. "If we were announcing our incoming presence, perhaps that would be a concern. But the unexpected can take out even the most powerful and prepared of sorcerers. Vituo, no matter how powerful he is, is still just a man at the end of the day. And all men bleed the same." Raj reassured. However, his wife still wasn't certain. "Look, if it makes you feel better let me go over exactly what the plan calls for again . . ."

8:30 AM Two Days Later:
Kidojoa

The attack had begun, and the entire city was just not prepared. Not for this, not for the Gimura Force to strike on the day the Crown Prince visited their humble city. They especially weren't prepared for this fearsome force of bandits to strike before their prince arrived; the city was practically defenseless as the band of outlaws ran rampant through the cleared streets. Sure, this aided the city defenders' response time, but the blitzkrieg and guerilla tactics of the tiny outlaw force proved more than a match for every single one of them.

The Gimura Force had attacked the city from five different angles in squads of ten. Jericho's team handled the east, Adam's team handled the west, Atto's team handled the south, and Penelope's team handled the north. Unfortunately, this left Raj and Imara to handle the main road, but not even the homely daughter's presence could bring Raj's mood down as the Gimura Force tore through the city in less than two hours, and with almost comical ease.

He had just made it to the city HQ when he received even better news, in the form of one of the panicking citizens. "Lord Vituo!

It's him!" one young woman yelled out, and as soon as she did, the citizens seemed to go quiet before breaking out in cheers.

"He's here! He'll save us all!" another yelled. Raj, Imara, and their team all turned and faced the direction the heartened citizens did. And standing before them was indeed the Crown Prince of the Masai Kingdom.

Imara felt her insides tingle at the sight of the young prince, and not just because she could faintly sense both the physical and political power he possessed. He was shorter than Jericho and Ron, but certainly taller than Raj and built like a true warrior prince. His jet-black dreadlocks flowed in the wind like a cape, yet also appeared to wreath his head in a mane-like fashion that made him seem like a king of beasts; fitting for what the Changelings that inhabited this and the other four Kingdoms of Paradise truly were. His brown skin and deep, earthen eyes further complemented his shoulder length locks, and said skin was complemented by the purple and teal imperial robes. The crown was almost unnecessary, for even if he were in rags there would be no doubt that he was a cut above the rest.

"So, you finally show yourself!" Raj barked out, pointing his trident at the young prince. Vituo however, was not perturbed in the least. "So, the reports were true after all, I see," he said, more to his royal guards and the priestess accompanying him than to anyone else. He then turned to his royal guards. "All of you, ensure the citizens get to safety, and then inform the Empress of the Elven Territories of what we found." He then turned to the priestess accompanying him. "Kyanna, you simply hang back; if I need back up, I'll signal for you." The prince grabbed his imperial robe, "Otherwise, I'll handle this."

Vituo threw off his imperial robes, revealing his purple and teal striped combat tights underneath. The black silk shirt was sleeveless, yet still bore the mark of the Chimera proudly on his chest in purple coloring. Imara had to look away to avoid staring at him further.

However, the Masai Prince simply continued to look at her; more specifically, to look at the weapon she wielded. "A Troll Scimitar? This is filthy rich coming from me of all people, but aren't you a little young to be a master sorceress?" Raj's eyes dilated in anger, hearing Vituo's words.

"Your fight is with me, Vituo!" Raj barked out.

However, Vituo simply ignored him as he addressed the priestess with him. "Kyanna, the girl. Search her chi." Kyanna did as she was told, her deep blue eyes glowing completely white as she did. Raj stepped in front of Imara.

"She's of no consequence. Your. Fight. Is. With. ME!" Raj said as he fired an energy blast at the prince. Vituo simply glared and dissipated the energy before it could get to him. In anger, Raj mustered all of his Physical chi, before unleashing it in one large, powerful ball of energy that he sent hurtling toward the Masai Prince. This time, however, he didn't make a move to stop it, as it harmlessly crashed into his chest.

It didn't even smudge the Chimera symbol on his silk shirt. "Hmph. This is all the leader of the Gimura Force has? I honestly expected more from a former general in the Elven Army." Vituo taunted, and Raj trembled from anger.

"Your highness, I don't sense any evil in her chi, or even a particular disturbance in the girl's mind." Kyanna interjected, her tone wary as she looked at Imara in what the prince knew was trepidation. He simply took in the words.

"Not even a sign that Troll's restraints are loosened?" he asked incredulously, as he stretched his legs and torso in preparation. Kyanna shook her head.

"No. The jewel in the hilt isn't even cracked or so much as fogged." Now, Vituo seemed very interested. In fact, he seemed to smile in anticipation.

"It's rare that I get to fight another young prodigy in the arts, let alone an unparalleled talent. But why is she serving this clown?" Raj heard the praise that Vituo spoke unto the disfavored daughter, and his hand clutched his trident in anger. As for Imara, she blushed at the compliment she had received from this handsome prince.

"Enough! I will not have my merit be compared poorly to this ugly failure!" With that, Raj charged at the Crown Prince, his double-edged trident swinging and spinning with murderous, yet very skilled intent. Raj's moves were perfect, but this just meant Vituo could perfectly predict his line of attack and dodge with the greatest of ease. Raj, getting more and more flustered, began to summon his physical aura to increase the speed and power of his slashes and twirls. However, Vituo began to chuckle.

"A former general in Empress Anmin's army, fallen to the level of a mere bandit. Obviously, your training has slacked, as well." Vituo's tone as he said this, as well as the fact that he dodged the faster and more powerful strikes in an even more nonchalant way just further angered Raj. With a powerful shout, Raj swung his trident with as much power as he could muster, leaving himself wide open for a very brutal retaliatory kick. Raj attempted to block it with his trident, but the weapon, his protective aura, and then his ribs were shattered like the weakest of glass as Vituo's kick sent Raj flying back. He slammed into one of the buildings and went limp.

"Dad!" Imara yelled, as she ran to him. Vituo made no move to stop her as she checked her fallen father's pulse, so the ten members of the Force rushing to defend the girl were unnecessary. She sighed in relief when she realized that he was simply out cold, but otherwise alive. "Thank goodness. Don't resist, please," she said, as she activated the Healer's Hand and began to restore him. Vituo and Kyanna both looked with interest.

Hmm . . . The Healer's Hand . . . Is she able to use the Living Triage technique? If so, this might be a while . . . Vituo mentally pondered.

I just have to distract them long enough, that's all . . . As he finished that thought, Kyanna spoke up.

"Your highness!" she exclaimed, and when Vituo followed her line of sight, he could see the rest of the Gimura Force converging, with who he presumed was Raj's family leading the charge.

"Dad!" Jericho and Hassan both exclaimed as they ran to where Imara was healing their still unconscious father.

"You're both dead!" Adam exclaimed, his broadsword pointed right at the Crown Prince and his priestess. Vituo was tempted to laugh; not one of the fifty-five bandits in front of him could perceive that it was they with the disadvantage, not him. However, he also perhaps admired their bravery. Imara finished healing her father, who had finally come to. He tried to stand, but his mind and body hadn't quite caught up to the beating he had just taken and then been revived from. The looks of concern on Penelope and Imara's faces said it all; Raj didn't even so much as jerk away from Imara as she tried to help him.

"Good, you're up. We need to retreat!" Atto said, signaling Ron to go assist his best friend.

"But . . . we have the young fool surrounded . . ." Raj managed to choke out, clearly still shaken up despite being healed.

"We need to retreat! The battle hasn't even begun yet, and you would have died had Imara not been here." Raj weakly growled at Ron's words; he wasn't able to muster any anger at the mention of his disfavored daughter at the moment. "We must simply live to fight another day. If we move now, we can outrun the reinforcements."

"How about this . . ." Vituo said, his voice causing every single member of the Gimura Force, except for Penelope, to form defensive formations and draw their weapons. He looked at Atto and Ron, then pointed to Imara. "The sorceress. She and I will duel for your right to retreat. Entertain me, and I just might let you all retreat with no dishonor or difficulty. The sorceress fights me alone, or else I will absolutely show none of you mercy. Is that clear?" Vituo posited, and now Raj found his energy.

"I will not place my life in the hands of this ugly failure!" Raj exclaimed.

Ron, however, held him back. "I'm not dying here. And neither is anyone else." Ron said with finality, his father concurring with him as well.

"Go on, Imara. You don't even have to win." Jericho said, his words hollowed out and unsure as he wondered if they should place their faith in the prince's words. "We'll be prepared to back you up, in case the prince's words are lies." Adam reassured. Imara took a tentative step forward, clutching the interesting weapon she wielded as though it were her only means of being saved. However, the final push she needed to steel her resolve and fight did not come from her allies.

"Hope you aren't as big a failure as your father thinks you are." Vituo taunted, crossing his arms behind his back. His words hung in the air for just a moment, the quiet before the storm.

And how the storm ensued, as Imara's trepidation was forgotten and she charged at the handsome prince with the worst intent. With both hands, she delivered some wicked slashes with her scimitar. Though Vituo dodged them as easily as he dodged Raj's attacks, he seemed more surprised at the change in Imara's demeanor than her skill with her weapon. Gone was the shy, deferential young woman; she was replaced with a warrior as fierce as any.

But Vituo wasn't just any warrior, as he dodged a particularly powerful slash and used his left hand to catch her hands. He almost disarmed her and broke her wrists on pure instinct and training, but decided instead to simply pull her through and throw her to the ground. She rolled through, and threw another particularly strong slash that, once again, left her wide open. This time, Vituo swept Imara's legs from under her. Imara landed with a thud, as the Masai Prince stood over her. "It's a rare occurrence that those who master sorcery also learn to hold their own in physical combat." Vituo complemented, but the cocky demeanor he possessed just really took away any genuine kudos he was giving. Imara responded in kind with an attempted sweep of her own, that Vituo of course dodged.

As he jumped back and allowed Imara the distance she needed, she took the opportunity to get back to her feet and fire off a few energy blasts. Vituo noted that they were quite a bit stronger than the blasts that Raj fired, but he was still able to deflect them with almost as much ease. That is, until he realized those blasts where actually diversions for Imara's real attack.

And that attack was a rather powerful flying kick, cloaked in the fiercest of Physical chi that Imara could summon. The energy formed itself into a dragon's head around the foot, and that head was way too close and far too fast for Vituo to just dodge it. The dragon roared on impact, and the roar drowned out the massive explosion that ensued. The sheer power of the explosion caused all of the spectators except for Kyanna to lose their footing. Some of the closer members of the Gimura Force, which included Imara's family, were blasted backward a good ten feet from the explosion.

Even Kyanna, despite not losing her vertical base in the slightest, had to cover her eyes from the projectile debris that the explosion kicked up. "Vituo!" She screamed, formalities all but forgotten as she felt the power of the impact and the Physical chi emitted from the explosion itself.

"We got him!? We took out the Masai Prince!" Raj celebrated. Penelope herself seemed to breathe a sigh of relief, as the Gimura brothers celebrated and cheered alongside their comrades at their apparent victory.

That is, until the dust cleared. Kyanna felt a great weight lift from her heart, at the same time the entire Gimura Force, especially

Penelope, felt their hearts sink. The silhouettes of two standing figures, black obviously before the dust completely cleared, but when it finally did the unthinkable became visible.

Vituo had caught Imara's Dragon Kick. A technique that she innovated and then further improved with the sole design to pierce through the strongest defenses. And Vituo had caught it with just one arm. "That . . . that's impossi . . . How did you . . ." Imara couldn't believe it herself. Kyanna, for her part, was speechless. Vituo, for just a moment, seemed nervous before regaining his composure.

"It's almost a shame that you will never reach your true potential," he said, with a bit of regret. Imara attempted to retract her leg, but Vituo was faster as he pulled her forward. With the same left hand, he used to pull her, he leveled her with one solid punch to the side of the face, sending her flying into what was left of the building they had been fighting in front of.

"No!" Penelope screamed.

If Vituo heard her, it only strengthened his resolve to kill the fallen prodigy. Imara could only sit helplessly as the Masai Prince gathered Lightning chi in his palm for what she knew was a killing blast. "Stop!" Penelope screamed again, this time moving forward before anyone could stop her. Imara's eyes dilated in horror at what her mother was doing.

But before she could say anything, Penelope did the unthinkable. She interfered in the duel; she raised her assault rifle and started firing. Vituo had looked up at just the moment Penelope had started firing, and though she herself was oblivious to his reaction, the others stared at the bullets dissipating in the lightning shield he summoned in just the nick of time with abject horror.

It was only after she had emptied the clip that she realized that not one of the bullets had the intended effect. Penelope trembled in a combination of fear and twisted joy at having saved her daughter, even if it meant her life was now on the line for it. "So, you choose to lay down your lives after all? Perhaps the Outlaw Code is alive and well," Vituo said, and Kyanna swore she heard a hint of respect etched into those words as he aimed the Lightning chi he had intended for Imara at Penelope.

Raj froze as the world seemed to slow down. He could not move, but his best friend and his sons certainly could. First Atto, then Hassan, and finally Adam, Jericho, Ron, and then the rest of the Force charged to Imara and Penelope's rescue.

For what it was worth, Imara and Penelope were saved, at the very least.

"Retreat! Penelope! Get out of there!" Raj called out, though noticeably his voice shook and he remained frozen where he was. The rest of the Gimura Force had rushed to Penelope and Imara's rescue, Hassan and then Atto leading the charge. Vituo turned, seeing the charging outlaws and taking his attention away from the two women. He looked to Kyanna.

"They choose death, priestess," he said, his order given, and the priestess descended to the ground. She remained hovering, which really just highlighted that Kyanna was only about five-foot-three on her best day and no heavier than 130 pounds. But from this small, lithe woman a serious amount of chi began to gather and then become compressed into a ball of pure power.

Penelope froze as she saw the ball of chi grow larger despite Kyanna compressing it down, but she took some comfort in knowing that she was shielding her daughter from the blast. Imara looked up, her eyes wide in terror. "Five different types of chi, in one powerful blast . . ." Imara said, clearly perturbed at the power of the priestess. Just as Kyanna released the ball of power, Imara had just barely finished conjuring Hajitar's Shield. Kyanna's attack slammed full force into the shield, and for what it was worth the shield protected her and Penelope very well. However, the answer to the question of what happens when an unstoppable attack meets an immovable defense was answered on this day.

Specifically, the attack simply disperses into an assault rain and scatters everywhere else. The screams of terror as everyone scrambled to dodge blurred together with the sound of Kyanna's spherical attack breaking apart. Adam, Jericho, and Hassan barely managed to dodge the blasts themselves, and Raj was simply out of range. However, Atto took the opportunity to try and close the distance. Kyanna was building up power for another chi blast, and that was perhaps why she failed to notice Atto until the moment his fist crashed into her face, knocking her cold. He pointed his spear at Vituo, who simply narrowed his eyes.

"You heard Master Maharajan! All of you! Retreat!" Atto commanded, to Ron's horror.

"But Dad!" Ron protested, and Atto made the mistake of taking his eyes off of the Masai Crown Prince.

"GO NOW!" Atto commanded. Ron's eyes teared up as he hesitated. He didn't want to leave his father behind, but even he had to know that numbers weren't going to make much of a difference at this point.

"Fifty lives for the price of one? Hmm . . ." Vituo pondered, before looking to Raj and the rest of the Gimura Force. "I suggest you retreat now. If you do, this man's sacrifice will not be in vain."

There was no taunting, mockery, or sarcasm in the Crown Prince's voice. He seemed almost . . . genuinely saddened by what he was about to do. He looked at Imara one last time. "Well? What are you waiting for?" With this, Vituo summoned up some Lightning chi. Upon glimpsing the sight of the Crown Prince gathering his power, Raj seemed to unfreeze and turned to run. The sight of their commander in full retreat caused the rest of the Force to retreat, with Ron and Imara both hesitating. Vituo didn't fire his attack; he simply waited for Atto's final words to his son.

"Ron, what are you still doing here?" Ron hesitated at his father's words. "I've made my decision. As I have my whole life. For once, no one else in my clan besides me should pay for it. Please, for just this once, do what your mother wouldn't. Save yourself, and live your life, not the life I forced you into." Once again, Ron hesitated, and this time Imara almost literally pulled him away. Ron was unable to resist; feeling his soul hollowing out and his physical willpower draining, he was simply a spectator in his own body as Imara pulled him away.

Leaving Atto to face his fate.

4:00 PM:
The Borderlands between the Elven Territories and the Kingdoms of Paradise

Ron and Imara finally reunited with rest of the Gimura Force; everyone, except for one, had made it out scuffed but alive. All except for the most important one, at least in Ron's mind. "Everyone got out unscathed? Did we lose anyone else? If not, tomorrow we march on the next target." Raj commanded, but then the unexpected happened, as Ron stepped up.

"We just lost the most important person on this force, and you think we're just going to move on with your worthless little plans as if nothing happened?!" Ron challenged, squaring up to the smaller yet more experienced warrior.

"Is that going to be a problem, Ron?" At that, even Penelope was tempted to step in, but Ron simply got closer. At six-two and a solid two hundred and fifty pounds of muscle, he was visibly taller and stronger than Raj.

"What if it is?" Ron challenged lowly. Raj was perhaps going to actually swing at the younger, bigger fighter, until Hassan spoke up.

"Dad, Atto is likely dead. Can't we—" to this, Raj cut off his son.

"Atto would want me to continue to fight and win, for not just my own sake, but to honor our friendship." Raj declared, and perhaps he even believed his own lie. But Ronmaru was the deceased's son; how dare Raj even give a pretense that he could ever know Atto better than his own family would.

"You have no right whatsoever to declare yourself a friend of my father's! When ALL you've ever done was cause him no end of trouble and leave him to clean up your mess!" Ron's voice cracked as the tears began to flow. At this, Imara, Hassan, and Jericho came to Ron's comfort. Raj looked to the rest of his Force; the solemn and mournful look on even Penelope's face perhaps told him what the right decision would have been.

But the looks of dissension and anger toward him from his men informed the decision Raj actually made. "Your father died so that your leader and future Emperor could live and continue to build the future he deserves. Don't let your mournful feelings cloud your judgment." Raj said, and at these words, Ron was reminded of Atto's final words to him, just a few hours ago.

Ron did not look up at him. "You're right, Master Maharajan. I can't let my feelings cloud my judgment," he said calmly. And Raj bought it.

"Good, now let's get ready to scout the next city," he said, and then made the mistake of turning his back.

Almost as soon as he took a step forward, Ron's fist collided with the back of the Gimura patriarch's head.

Forty-Five Minutes Later

Raj was awake; at least he thought he was. His vision was still black, but he knew he was no longer dreaming, for he felt the ropes around his ankles and wrists. Upon feeling his restraints, he realized he must have been blindfolded. And that could only mean . . .

"You miserable, filthy ingrates! Is this a mutiny? A rebellion?!" Raj roared out, though the echo that sounded indicated he was in the hostage convoy. Even if someone could hear him, they could easily just tune him out. "HEY! I'm your best chance at survival, ALL OF YOU! Atto is DEAD! I'm the last one who can negotiate with any nobility! Let me out of here!" Raj yelled out authoritatively, but even he had to hear the twang of fear under his voice. No response was given to him, and this just made him thrash about more. "HEY! You can't do this! Let me out of here!" he pleaded, once again to no avail. However, just a few moments later, he noticed that the vehicle had stopped.

We've stopped, he observed, before he heard talking outside. Is . . . is that . . .? Raj knew that voice; he knew that voice really well. He didn't know whether to be flattered or in abject terror and awe, but he was going to make himself heard in any case. "General

Tensai?! Is that you?" Almost as soon as he said this was the moment he heard the hatch open, and then perceived the feeling of being picked up. When he was set down, his blindfold was removed . . .

And there stood General Persimmon Tensai. Raj never thought he'd see him again, least of all as a bounty that was now being collected. Raj would have jumped to his feet if they weren't bound; his anger at his former rival was palpable. "General," Ronmaru's voice sounded, and to Raj's surprise it was devoid of aggression. In fact, not one member of the Gimura Force, not even his family, made a move against what should have been one of the most valuable targets in the Elven Military. They looked almost as though they were about to do the unthinkable.

"What are you doing?! He's all alone! Kill him!" Ron almost laughed; he couldn't believe Raj still thought he had any sort of command or control at this point. However, Raj looked right at Imara; she was clearly doing her best to ignore her father, but even an amateur could see her nervousness. "Imara! Stop being a damned failure and prove your worth, for once! Help me! Kill him and help your father!" Raj barked out, though the desperation continued to creep into his voice. Imara squeezed her eyes shut, but Raj wasn't having any hesitation. "Damn you, you ugly failure! Will you abandon your father!? Have you no gratitude!" Imara teared up, and even Tensai's expression softened for just a moment. However, Ron brought his foot down on Raj's skull, knocking him out cold again.

"What Raj meant to say in all of that . . ." Ron started as he turned to the Elven General. Perhaps there was something just a bit comical about the six-two, solidly built warrior bowing to the five-five older man, but the other members of the Gimura Force followed his example. "We unconditionally surrender. Our battle and our coup against the Elven Territories end now." Ron said solemnly. He did not see General Tensai give a signal; Imara was the last to bow and was the only one able to see it as a result.

"The Masai Prince informed us that both Maharajan Gimura and Attoullichos Jotomatu were sighted in one of his border cities. Where is your father?" Tensai asked, but Ron simply did not answer or even so much as look up from his kowtowing position.

The general didn't need an answer. The tears rolling down Ron's face was more than enough to spell out Atto's fate. "Attendant Jotomatu will be sorely missed. He was loyal and his skills with sorcery were invaluable to her Majesty's forces. Until he revolted . . ." Tensai said, glowering at the unconscious Raj. However, his face became unreadable when he cast his eyes on the rest of the Gimura family. Imara's spine turned to ice when she met his gaze; she and her mother were the only females her father had allowed in the Gimura Force and his lingering gaze made her skin crawl. "You . . . Where is your weapon?" Tensai asked, and Imara shuddered as she tentatively answered.

"It's . . . it's in the vehicle I arrived in." Tensai nodded, changing his body language as he made another signal. "Take me to it. And as for the rest of you . . ." As he spoke, some troops teleported onto the scene. Some used Fire chi, others used Water chi, still some used Lightning chi, a few used Earth chi, and there was even a couple who used Wind chi. The lower ranking troops present used good old fashioned Physical chi for their teleportation, but the fact that they teleported using their chi was demonstration enough of at least intermediate use of chi. "Take the subordinate rebels to Havardina for judgment. I will personally hand-deliver Ronmaru Jotomatu and the Gimura family to her Majesty." He looked to Imara. "But first . . ." he said, and he need not say anymore.

Imara led Tensai and five of his trusted troops to the van she and her brothers had arrived in. In the passenger seat was her trusted weapon, newly shined and on full display. All five elites gasped in awe when they saw the Troll Scimitar; all but one of them took a tentative step back from Imara once they realized just how very real this mythical weapon was. "That . . . but she's so young . . ." The only elite warrior who didn't step back from Imara repeated the Masai Prince's words. It never occurred to her in all her years of wielding this weapon just why it made her special; it had always been a source of misfortune in her relationship with her father.

Tensai simply nodded. "So, the Changelings weren't fabricating their reports after all. And neither were the southern townships and villages." The diminutive general said. What he lacked in height he made up for in physical fitness, but Imara still suspected he was barely heavier than her. His powerful voice was a real contrast to his stature, but she could sense his chi about as well as any competent sorceress could. "Where did you find this?" he asked, to which Imara shrugged.

"I never found it, sir," she said meekly. "My father did, and he nearly went crazy when he wielded it. I was able to calm him down, and he let me have it ever since." She truthfully explained.

"You broke the inhabitant's control over the wielder. And then kept the same loss of control that your father experienced, from happening to you." Tensai pondered, before making a decision.

He picked up the scimitar. He actually grabbed the hilt and lifted the Troll Scimitar out of the passenger's seat, and was now holding it to inspect it. The five elites and Imara barely had time to gasp in utter terror before Tensai's eyes glowed orangish-red. He squeezed them shut and gritted his teeth for just a moment, but nothing he did could hold in his scream of agony as his body failed to resist the pink chi cloak that forced itself around the general. For a split second he tried to pry his hand from around the scimitar's hilt using his free hand, but he made no headway before his body went into throes and spasms as the Troll within the jewel began to start the process of taking hold of the general.

Where the five elites froze and were stumped at what to do, Imara acted. "Give me some room!" she said with urgency, as she grabbed the hilt of the Troll Scimitar with one hand as she braced the other on the chest of the seizing general fighting for his soul on the ground. In a few seconds, the pink cloak dissipated, and the jewel on the hilt of the scimitar was no longer glowing.

"Aww . . . Damn it! DAMN IT!" A voice sounded in both Imara and Tensai's heads. The voice of the Troll sealed in the offending scimitar. "I will be free! You can't keep me in here forever!" he warned as the jewel solidified again, cutting off the Troll's contact with the outside world. Tensai caught his breath, now completely free of the Troll's hold over him.

"General?" Imara asked meekly. Tensai sat up.

"Am . . . am I still alive?" he asked no one in particular as he checked to make sure he still had all of his limbs. He summoned some chi; his soul appeared intact.

"Sir, you were . . ." Tensai held up his hand to silence his subordinate. "There is but one way that you were able to free me and suppress the Troll housed in that jewel. But how? How did you learn to harness the necessary chi to do so?" he asked, and Imara simply shrugged.

"I just . . . always knew how, I guess." Imara really couldn't explain it. The general seemed to buy it, as he touched his C-Ring.

"Your Majesty? We found the reported wielder of the Troll Scimitar," Tensai said.

Imara suddenly got a really bad feeling in the pit of her stomach.

Empress Anmin's Capitol Castle, Madina, Almurkarzia, Elven Territories

"Mom?" a teenaged voice sounded, distracting the Empress from her call.

"Azuro, we'll be having some very special guests for you soon. Your sixteenth birthday will be sweet, indeed," she reassured in a singsong voice as she returned to her C-Ring. The Empress sounded exactly as one would expect a woman who has been pampered all of her life to sound.

"General, simply bring the prodigal sorceress to my palace. My ladies-in-waiting will take care of the rest," she said, and after hearing an affirmative she dismissed her subject. "Well, Azuro, you'll be happy to know you'll have another training partner. And maybe even another potential Empress for your reign," she said, her singsong voice returning. Azuro simply rolled his eyes.

"Mom, come on. I told you, there's time for that later. Right now, I just need to focus on my studies and—" the Empress simply laughed, interrupting her son.

"Son, your reign won't be until I pass away, and that won't be any time soon," she reassured. However, Azuro shook his head.

"But what if you want to retire one day? Wouldn't you want to know that your kingdom is in good hands once you do?" he asked in concern, to which the Empress simply shrugged.

"You're just like your grandfather, which I guess is a good thing for the future of our dynasty. But you don't want to end up like your brother, now do you?" she asked, to which Azuro tensed.

"Mom, Syn wasn't wrong on all things. A good Emperor starts as a studious prince, and a studious prince starts as a dutiful son—" Azuro said, before the Empress cut him off.

"—and ends up passing away before his children reach adulthood," the Empress certainly knew how to stop a conversation with her son cold. And if the Empress's goal was to make herself and her son sad, she more than achieved that as well. Mother and son simply resumed training without a word for the rest of the day.

The Next Morning:
Gimura Force Hideout

As Imara put on her clothes, she observed her reflection for the last time before she put on her t-shirt and shorts. She really was quite well-endowed, which was not a surprise given Penelope was her mother. The very enticing purple lingerie she wore tastefully covered her, but was quite provocative in what it showed off, nonetheless. Her chest and curves in general were quite a bit bigger than her mother's, mostly on account of Imara herself being slightly taller and heavier anyway. Even her full, pink lips were perhaps attractive enough, if only her sharp nose, pointed ears and reptilian yellow eyes weren't above said lips. She wondered why she alone was born less beautiful than the rest of her family, almost as much as she wondered why she alone possessed the mystical talent that she did.

When she finished dressing, Imara looked at her weapon; almost out of force of habit she began to clean it to the specifications Raj would have expected during the sound offs. It was only after she finished cleaning her weapon that she remembered that she'd never again have to deal with her father's inane pretentions toward military bearing. "Good riddance . . ." Imara angrily hissed out to no one in particular, but she quickly became embarrassed that she said that aloud as though an audience had heard her and gasped in shock at her words.

She did not know why, but she still respected her father. She was fully aware of his toxic personality and knew that in general Raj was a real downer whenever he was around. Yet, Imara wondered if the right thing wasn't to take Ron and her remaining family and attempt to stage Raj's escape. A part of her felt that all of her family deserved her loyalty, yet most of her knew Raj would never have done the same for her.

Her thoughts were interrupted once she stepped into the main room of the Hideout. "To think, this place seems almost . . . domesticated." It was Tensai who spoke, and in the massive, empty hideout his voice was very conspicuous in how it carried. It almost seemed wrong for this hideout to have less than fifty people occupying it at a time; Imara never noticed it until now, but her father's hideout was truly designed with fifty or more recruits in mind.

"Yeah, Raj didn't plan on it, but we wound up living here for eight years. We were well hidden, as you might have guessed by now." Ron recounted, though there was clearly a hint of sadness to his voice. Tensai continued his impromptu tour of the place, clearly committing everything to memory as he did. "Raj would always talk about how one day he'd found his own dynasty and right the wrongs of this current crown, with my father as his Chancellor of course. I don't know why, but Dad always believed in him. He always believed Raj was soon to become Emperor, even as the garage got added. Even as more and more decorations and domestications were added to this little cave. Soon enough, it became the mansion and permanent residence you see before you." Ron continued, and just how little headway Raj made in his eight years of leading the Gimura Force really sunk in for Imara as he said this.

Tensai was about to say something, until he saw Imara. His mouth gaped in place for a moment as his eyes practically feasted on her body in her civilian clothes. His shorter height just made it so obvious that his eyes went right to her legs and hips, which were shown off quite well in her gray skirt. She didn't show cleavage; she did not need to, for the outline of her ample breasts were enough of a reminder of their presence under her black shirt. Imara's face flushed red in embarrassment, for this was the second man to be surprised at what she had hidden under her armor. "Umm . . . General?" Adam said, clearly perturbed at the way Tensai looked at Imara. Tensai shook his head.

"My apologies. I was just . . . lost in thought on yet another thing Raj was wrong about," he said, tearing his eyes away from Imara's body. "We should really get going," Tensai said, and was quick to cut the tour short. Adam, Jericho, and Hassan looked to one another.

"Well, that was creepy as all hell," Hassan said what the older Gimura brothers were thinking, to which Ron simply chuckled.

"Again, Raj thinks she's unattractive?" he reiterated, hoping someone would finally agree with him outright. No one did, as Raj's very name seemed to dampen the mood a bit.

One Hour Later:
Almukarzia Imperial Highway

Imara was lost in thought as she looked at the scenery pass by; it had been eight years since she had seen her birth province. Raj and the Gimura Force did not dare venture into the heart of the Elven Territories; not until the day they'd be ready to seize the crown. After two years of stagnated progress, Imara simply resigned herself to never seeing her hometown again unless it was in a prison convoy. She never in her life suspected she'd be in the passenger seat of a Royal Guest's convoy to the Empress's palace. Even nobility who weren't disgraced would rarely travel down this immaculate path. The vehicle was as luxurious as one would expect, but Imara really wasn't enjoying it as she should.

Her mind kept going back to the fact that Tensai took her brothers and Ron to Havardina, alongside the rest of the Gimura Force. And she knew exactly what fate was awaiting her father; she couldn't shake the feeling that her mother, brothers, and best friend would all be charged as accomplices to her father's coup. She wondered why she alone was meeting the Empress and her inner circle, until she remembered the weapon just under her seat. The weapon that angered her father to no end, the weapon she and she alone seemed able to wield with no ill effects. She had saved her father's life in much the same way she had saved General Tensai, but Imara couldn't help but wonder if some of Hajitar's influence didn't linger in her father's mind.

In either case, the convoy entered Madina. Which meant that Imara would know her fate soon enough . . .

1:00 PM:

The Empress's Palace, Meditation Garden

The Empress's C-Ring glowed, indicating that her last Royal Guest had entered the palace. "Wonderful. The guest of honor has finally showed up." Anmin said in her characteristic sing-song voice. "Make sure she is bathed and given presentable and appropriate dress. She will be expected to join us at 5:00. Not a minute later. Until then, treat her as though she is a member of the Royal Family," she ordered.

Given that her Chancellor, Grand Marshal, Grand Priest, and quite a few high-level officials from her Imperial Court were present. "The daughter of Maharajan Gimura? Shouldn't she be joining her family for judgment?" one official asked.

"She's the one who can wield a Troll Scimitar and survive, isn't she?" another official asked, a hint of fear in her voice at the statement.

"I'll believe that when I see it," a very skeptical older minister scoffed. A younger minister gave him a look of shock and incredulity. "But what if the Grand Priest can't see the Troll in time when it escapes?" he asked, his voice quavering.

"A single Troll surely can't stand against the Grand Priest and the entire Sanctorum, can he?" another posited, though even he sounded unsure of this suggestion.

However, it was one of the Grand Priest's students who ultimately silenced them all. "Don't forget, that I am the next Grand Priest! And while I am here, whoever this sorceress is will ensure that Troll of hers stays in her weapon." The looks from the Empress, Crown Prince, Chancellor, and Grand Marshal said it all, but the Grand Priest was the one to speak up.

"Torune, I'm sure she's not a threat to any of us if she's submitting to be brought before the Imperial Court like this. But you make a point. In case she doesn't accept the Empress's offer, you are free to do as you please. Consider it live training for what you'll have to do once I step down."

Having heard that, the Santorum's best student nodded. "Hmph," he said, as he calmed down. The rest of the Imperial Court rolled their eyes at the young man's boasts, as the Empress dismissed them to prepare for the 5:00 gathering.

5:00 PM:
The Empress's Palace, the Reception Hall

Imara's body was still sore all over from the "bath" she received almost four hours ago; she could now give firsthand sympathy to the unfortunate commoners and low-level nobles her father spoke about in his stories. Especially those who received the wire brush bathing; she wondered how the burly, mannish maids didn't draw blood when they were harshly scrubbing her with the automated cleaning tool. It still stung a bit to walk, but even Imara had to admit that she felt and smelled a lot cleaner now than she ever did even before her father's coup. Not to mention that the clothes she wore felt lighter and more luxurious than anything she ever wore during her exile. Even ugly failures can fool others into believing she's something more if she dresses above her birth. Imara found herself thinking, until she realized she let herself think of her father's usual words to her.

She closed her yellow snake-like eyes for a moment; she must not allow her mind to waver. Not in front of the Imperial Court, not if she was to help her family out of their predicament. Almost as soon as Imara let out her breath did the doors open and reveal just who she'd be training with from the Empress's Imperial Court. In the center, sitting on the throne above everyone else was none other than the Empress herself. And though Empress Malkia Anmin was exactly as Imara remembered her to be, now more than ever could Imara assess the person who wore the crown.

Imara swore that the dress she herself was given was more luxurious than the one the Empress herself wore. In fact, the Empress and the Crown Prince were the least opulently dressed of everyone present, though Imara could never recall there being a rule about formal dress being required. In general, Imara noticed the relaxed, lounging, and perhaps unladylike posture of the Empress as well as the friendly, warm smile on her beautiful face as the daughter of the disgraced County Chief entered the reception hall. Her posture emphasized her hourglass figure; her hips and legs were bigger in person than they were in the picture her father showed her, but the Empress otherwise looked exactly like the beautiful ebony-haired princess in the picture her father would always show the rest of the family.

Sitting to her right was definitely her son Azuro; Imara was surprised at how young he was, given all that she heard of him. He seemed stern and quite serious; the Crown Prince's glare was as intimidating as Vituo's, despite him likely being younger than even she was. Imara wondered if Azuro looked more like his mother when he smiled, because right now he almost definitely resembled his father with his glower. Azuro narrowed his eyes, which was all the prompting Imara needed. "Your majesties," she greeted with a bow, to which Empress Anmin laughed.

"An Empress's Guest of Honor is treated as though she is her equal. No need for formalities, Imara," she reminded the nervous teen, to which Azuro rolled his eyes. "Come, join us," she prompted, directing Imara to the seat just to Empress Anmin's left.

Imara looked around, her face flushing red at the looks she was receiving from the nobles and high-level officials as they waited to see what she was going to do. Imara simply refused to look at them as she walked forward, but unfortunately this now meant she was very much looking at Malkia's three younger siblings. The imperial princes were much like Azuro, in that they were unsmiling and seemed quite unwelcoming of most, let alone the daughter of the traitor. Imara could not read their expressions, which only further intimidated her as she made her way to the empty seat.

She did her best to hide her nervousness as all eyes went right to her. She crossed her legs and breathed a sigh of relief when she noticed quite a few eyes were no longer on her own as a result. "Tell me, sweetheart. How old are you?" the Empress asked conversationally, and Imara did her best to focus on the Empress and none of the other officials or the imperial princes.

"I . . . I'm seventeen, your majesty," Imara stammered out. Anmin looked out to the audience; everyone realized at that moment and softened their expressions without needing to be prompted further.

"Don't worry, just answer truthfully, sweetheart," the Empress reassured, though it was clearly an unspoken order given to the imperial princes and her officials.

She turned back to Imara. "Now, you're Maharajan's daughter, aren't you? His only one, if I'm not mistaken. What's your name?" Imara swallowed, feeling a little more confident now.

"Imara. My name is Imara," she said, hoping the Empress would continue on the subject of her family. She did not have to hope for long.

"Your father caused my Court and my subjects no end of trouble in the eight years his rebel force was active. Maharajan always had a talent for leadership and war. Tell me, how did you come to possess a Troll Scimitar?" she asked. Imara noticed that the Grand Priest and the other officials who represented the Elven Church now had their interests piqued, but for a different reason. She noticed one in particular looked as though hearing the utterance of the words "Troll Scimitar" alone made him fighting mad. However, a glare from the Empress told all present that any comments and questions needed to be held until she and Imara finished their conversation.

"My family just found it one day and brought it back to our hideout. When Dad tried to hold it . . ." Imara began to tear up at the memory of that horrible day. The members of the Elven Church gasped; others shared in the moment with Imara. Quite a few of them didn't even need to know the details of the incident Imara mentioned, but she continued anyway. "My mother, my brothers, and Ron, they are the only people I have left from that day," Imara pleaded, and it wasn't lost on the Empress that Imara managed to beg for her family's life despite the painful memory. The Empress would inform the young girl of her family's clemency soon enough.

Right now, the Empress needed answers. "How did you survive? What did you do?" Anmin asked, to which Imara simply looked at her with a vulnerable look in her snake-like eyes.

"Your majesty, I really don't know what I did to save him. I sensed that the Troll within the jewel was using Physical, Elemental, and Spirit chi to take over my father's body, so I just summoned as much of those chi as I could and grabbed the weapon. I don't know why that worked, but it just . . . did. I saved my father's life and the lives of those who remained, and they kind of just let me keep it from then on." Imara said as innocently and truthfully as she could. She wondered if anyone present believed her.

"You balanced Physical, Elemental, and Spirit chi? And used them at once effectively?" Azuro finally spoke for the first time, betraying his surprise and awe at what Imara just told him.

"Ye . . . yes, your majesty," she said nervously, realizing everyone was looking at her once again. Empress Anmin didn't stop them this time; she too was looking at Imara in a new light. The Grand Priest spoke up.

"Who taught you? Was it a rogue from the Sanctorum? Or was it Synturo Anmin?" he questioned, and the blank look on Imara's face perhaps told him the answer before her words did.

"I swear, I don't know of any rogue elements to this Imperial Court besides my father and Atto. I wasn't taught how to do any of this. I just learned on my own from studying," Imara pleaded, and perhaps the rest of the Imperial Court sensed the truth of her statement.

Imara tried not to look at the seething young sorcerer seated next to the Grand Priest. That is, until she noticed some chi building up in his hand.

And by the time she did, it was too late, for he had already pointed his two fingers and fired a ray of energy at her. Even the Grand Priest looked shocked at the sudden action, and Imara closed her eyes in fear as she almost reflexively conjured up a shield. But not just any shield; the pink aura indicated that she had summoned Hajitar's Shield. Malkia and Azuro were perhaps more shocked at the fact Imara summoned this barrier than at what the Grand Priest's hot-headed student did. And just in time, too; the ray of energy collided with the barrier with a thunderous crash that echoed throughout the reception hall.

"Hmph!" the student said, seemingly happy that he invoked a fearful response from the prodigal sorceress that dared to take up his spotlight.

"Torune!" the Grand Priest yelled out, perhaps shocking Torune back to Earth.

But right then, something went wrong. Oh, so very wrong. Just as soon as the shield was summoned and Torune admired his handiwork did a blinding blast of light burst into his vision. His eyes burned from the light, and he fell backward from the docket he sat in. He screamed as he convulsed and flailed on the floor, feeling his eyes boil and bubble from the blast of light. "MY EYES! SHE'S BLINDED ME! THAT UGLY BITCH BLINDED ME," Torune screamed, the fear and pain in his voice apparent.

"Calm down! Hold still!" Torune heard, but that was much easier said than done. That is, until he felt really powerful hands on his shoulders and legs, and then a hand was placed over his eyes. As the pain in his eyes eased, Torune began to calm down a bit more until the pain went away entirely.

"Ah . . . Am I . . .?" he asked, but then his vision was entirely restored. And when it was, he was greeted with the angry faces of most of the Imperial Court. None, however, were angrier than Azuro and the Grand Priest.

"Are you insane!?" Azuro asked incredulously. The Grand Priest got closer to his highest-ranked student, pushing the healer aside. "This. Is. TREASON! What would you have done if that blast had hit the Empress OR the Crown Prince?! Do you think Atomic chi is a toy to play carelessly with?!" Torune backed away from the shorter, much older man, with what looked like abject fear. "You IMBECILE!! Just like EVERY. SINGLE. MEMBER. Of your WORTHLESS CLAN! WE GIVE YOU CHANCES, AND THIS IS HOW YOU REPAY US!? YOU DAMNED FOOL! ALL OF MY TIME AND CARE, AND YOU THROW IT ALL AWAY! FOR WHAT?! WELL?" The Grand Priest seethed, no longer able to say words. Torune himself seemed at a loss for words; he himself realized that he just acted before he thought. There really wasn't a good explanation for what he just did. That is, until he looked at the offending prodigal sorceress sitting next to the Empress.

If Torune was going to blame Imara, Azuro never gave him a chance. "Mother, you told me to give my father's clan a chance to prove themselves worthy. Well, does anyone here think Torune doesn't deserve the death penalty?" the Crown Prince asked, and hearing those words made Torune's eyes dilate with fear.

"Wait, you can't!" he simpered out, now realizing exactly how much trouble he was now in. The Grand Priest scoffed.

"Oh, yes we can. And yes, we shall. NO LOW-CLASS SCUM WILL EVER PULL A STUNT LIKE THAT EVER AGAIN!" With that, the Grand Priest and his other students powered up their chi blasts.

Before Torune could simper and beg yet again, the Empress spoke up. "ENOUGH!" she called out, getting everyone's attention as she jumped to her feet. Azuro stared at his mother incredulously.

"But . . . Mom . . ." Azuro attempted, but Malkia was hearing none of it.

"Azuro, stand down." She then looked at the Grand Priest sternly. "You too, Gari. That's enough!" At hearing his name being said, the Grand Priest hesitated for just a moment before relenting and letting his chi blast die on his hand.

"Mom, you can't possibly let Torune's outburst go unpunished!" Malkia simply laughed; Imara noted that it seemed that only the Crown Prince dared to argue with the Empress thus far. She wondered what would have happened if even the Grand Priest or the Grand Marshal had tried to get a word in edgewise.

"Who said he was going unpunished?" the Empress said. If Torune had breathed a sigh of relief, he immediately tensed back up upon hearing that.

"If not an execution, then how, pray tell, do you plan to do it?" Azuro asked, unable to remove the snarky tone from his words.

"My boy, you will find that execution is really a wasteful punishment to levy. Especially when you can do oh so much worse," she responded, and now she looked at the trembling Torune.

"Torune, I saw the way you looked at Imara. I could see the anger in your eyes when I asked her to join me and my son. So much rage and jealousy, at someone you don't even know." She shook her head. "It is definitely time for you to learn that you can't just act out like this. Until you do, though, Imara will be the next Grand Priestess." Imara's mouth dropped open upon hearing this, as did the Grand Priest and the other high-level officials of the Elven Church. Torune's eyes filled with tears at hearing the loss of his opportunity. He couldn't stand anymore, so he fell back into his seat as his legs gave way.

"But . . . I'm sorry . . ." he said, though even he perhaps knew how weak he sounded right about now.

"Your majesty?" the Grand Priest almost dumbly asked, but the Empress once again seized control of the situation.

"Of course, Gari and the other priests will give you the training you need. But I think with your talent for sorcery, and other strengths that you will soon discover you possess, my son will have a solid Grand Priestess when his reign begins," Malkia declared, and now Azuro chimed in.

"But what of him?!" Azuro asked, pointing to the Grand Priest's former successor. To which the Empress laughed jovially.

"Oh, he can tell his friends that Imara is now in charge of the Sanctorum, given she's the new successor to the Grand Priest." His eyes hardened again, though the tears now flowed freely.

"If you just want me to commit suicide, just order it! You don't need to gaslight or mentally torture me!" Torune yelled out, earning yet another glare from the Church officials. Azuro smirked at this outburst.

"Get him out of here. And back to his equals." Azuro was clearly taunting the former successor, and as the guards led Torune out of the reception hall, the Empress turned to Imara.

"Before you go to the Sanctorum, is there anything you need to get your training started?" she asked.

Imara was not about to let this opportunity pass her by.

8:00 AM the Next Morning:
The Imperial Palace,
Imara's Suite

Imara almost didn't want to get out of bed; the luxurious bed she slept in ensured that it was the most rest she'd gotten in her entire life. Even before she was expected to fight, Imara could not remember knowing comfort like this.

No! I can't think of the past anymore. Imara thought as she got out of bed and prepared for her day. And just as soon as she decided what to wear did her C-Ring beep. Even the sound the C-Ring made was more pleasant than C-Rings her father had given the family, and it was as Imara answered it that she realized just how difficult moving on from the past would actually be. "Good morning, your majesty," she said, expecting to hear Empress Anmin's voice.

"How are you feeling this morning?" The young, masculine voice greeted from the other side. Azuro's voice. Imara blinked, before answering.

"I'm . . . okay . . ." she said, not quite sure why he wasn't as uptight and imperious as he was yesterday.

"The requests you made. They've been fulfilled," he said gently, though noticeably he was unable to remove the imperious undertone for his words. Either way, Imara's eyes lit with excitement.

"Are they here now?" she asked hopefully, and Azuro rewarded her faith.

"Right here in front of me. Waiting on you to join us for breakfast," he said.

Imara didn't waste any time. In five minutes, she was being escorted to the Dining Hall. They were simultaneously the shortest and the longest five minutes of her life, because she couldn't be reunited with her family and friend fast enough. They hadn't even started eating yet; they had been waiting for her to join them. "She listened to me? She let them go?" Imara said incredulously, and she saw the kindly look upon Azuro's face. Imara ran right past the Grand Priest and his subordinate sorcerors and immediately fell into the embrace of her friend and her family. After a few moments of reunion, they sat down to eat.

It was noticed that everyone except Raj was present. "Where's Dad?" she asked Penelope, who noticeably paused when Imara asked that question. She then looked to her brothers, who all noticeably either sipped their tea, took a bite of food, or otherwise engaged in a clear I'm not gonna be the one to say it behavior. Ron, however, shrugged.

"Imara . . . Well, there's no easy way to say this . . ." he said, and Imara's snake-like eyes dilated.

"Is he . . .?" she asked, to which Azuro tilted his head.

"That man has done nothing but cause you, your family, and your friends no end of trouble. Especially you; how can you stand to be around him when all he does is hurt, abuse, and misuse you and force you to waste your talents away?" To this, Imara squeezed her eyes shut, hoping to suppress her emotions before opening them to look at Azuro as she spoke.

"He's my father. He's the only father I have. Family, at the end of the day, is family. And what kind of person would I be to not try all I could to defend my family?" Imara said in what she hoped was a confident voice.

Even if it was, Azuro's face softened. Now Imara prepared for the worst, for it was the Grand Priest who stepped up to deliver the news. "You're a woman of much character, I'll give you that. But unfortunately, the Empress has ruled that Maharajan Gimura is too treacherous and dangerous to be allowed amnesty. That is the only request of yours that she will not fulfill." A look of grief came over Imara's face as she looked down.

Mourning someone like Raj, even after all he's done to her, Azuro thought, as he finally looked at the rest of Imara for the first time. Before he let his eyes wander too far, he steeled his mind to continue to look her in the face. Penelope and her sons simply shared in the moment with Imara, even if they didn't quite agree with her on whether Raj deserved her sympathy. After a moment, Azuro felt it was time.

"Imara, you are part of the Imperial Court, and my Inner Circle now. I understand what you're going through, but you will fulfill your orders. And you will complete your training with the Grand Priest," Azuro said sternly, his eyes firmly locked on Imara's as he kept his voice steady. "As soon as we're done here, your training with the Grand Priest will begin. As will yours." Azuro looked at Ron as he said this. "The Empress informed me that you made a special request." Azuro was a machine right now; the Grand Priest almost smirked at how differently from the Empress the son handled his own Inner Circle.

Ron bowed. "Her majesty said she'd find my old weapon and have an Earth Teleporter built into it," Ron said as respectfully as he could. Azuro simply turned to look at Torune and the rest of the Sanctorum.

"Present it," he said simply, and Torune was happy that he wasn't the one assigned to that duty. The two largest, strongest members of the Sanctorum struggled and strained as they brought the weapon in question into view. It was just as Ron remembered it; the shining black great sword was clearly kept in pristine condition. Even the ribs on the purple hilt were kept impeccably grooved and individualized; there was not a single blend or other sign of dulling. A few seconds of watching the two men struggle with carrying his weapon passed before Ron simply held out his hand.

"Guess now is as good a time as any," he said, as he summoned some Earth chi to his hand. And when he focused it at the hilt, his weapon teleported to his hand and relieved the two warriors who could only amble and shuffle slowly while they carried the massive blade.

Torune and his friends were visibly shocked at the fact that Ron held this five-hundred-pound weapon with just one hand. "Ah yes. Did you miss me, sweetheart?" he asked his weapon as he rubbed the blade with his free hand. "If you could all give me a minute," Ron asked, and Azuro motioned for everyone to stand back. As soon as they did, Ron promptly began to demonstrate just what he remembered from his days of wielding this weapon.

Beginning from the first and most basic sword kata, he then seamlessly transitioned to harder and more complex demonstrations until he reached the tenth and most difficult kata taught to swordsmen. Ron never once lost the equalization between his focus, balance, precision of strikes, power, and especially his technique. Torune and his former subordinates were visibly in awe and in fear at not only Ron's technical prowess, but also the fact that he performed these katas and demonstrations as if the five-hundred-pound great sword in his hand were the ten-pound training sword given to beginners.

Imara and her family were awed for a different reason. "I'm surprised you remembered all of that," Adam said as soon as Ron was done and took a relaxing breath. Ron chuckled when he heard Adam's words.

"Once you learn, it never leaves you. It felt good to finally have a weapon in my hand again." Ron held the sword over his head, fully extending his arm. "Now, it feels like I could do actual damage if I'm not careful. I'm scared to let my grip slip now. Unlike those rigid noodles Raj called spears. Or the sharp sticks he considered swords," Ron said, his face betraying his disgust at how light his spear had been during his time on the Gimura Force.

Imara turned to the youthful prince. "See why I requested him so? I think Ron's more than capable of being a competent second in command," Imara said, to which Ron nodded. However, Torune became incensed when he heard this, and promptly stepped forward.

"Are you serious?" he exclaimed, once again losing his temper. "You mean to tell me I don't even get to keep a secondary position in the Sanctorum?!" Torune complained, to which Azuro simply glared at him. Torune pointedly looked away from Azuro to continue ranting.

"Since when does she get to decide who outranks whom?" He might have kept going, but the Grand Priest teleported in front of him.

"Since yesterday, when you did exactly this same thing in Imperial Court." The older man was clearly losing patience with his disgraced student. Ron, for his part stepped up and was likely going to meet Torune with violence had the Grand Priest not stopped him. "You did this to yourself. I don't know how you Mujins act back home in your old village, but I warned you from the start not to bring that uncouth behavior to the Imperial Court. Like it or not, you all will listen to Priestess Gimura, and follow her orders the first time," the Grand Priest said sternly. The rest of Torune's friends within the Sanctorum shared his anger at these words. They might have even stepped up to help the friend who had secured their positions within this elite group of sorcerers, if only they weren't outnumbered and outmatched in more ways than just magically.

Torune scoffed. "Hmph, whatever. But you!" Torune immediately pointed to Imara, who pursed her lips in shock at being singled out. "Don't ever try to blind me again! Don't even so much as use Illusion Conversion around me, not ever again!" he barked out viciously. The plaintive look on Imara's face made Ron seethe.

"As the leader of the Sanctorum, it's my duty to ensure no one under my charge ever comes to harm. Now that we're allies, I see no reason to use Illusions on you any longer," Imara explained, keeping her voice level and soft in hopes she could diffuse the situation. It didn't, as Torune seemed to get madder.

"Just remember, I wouldn't mind boiling off that ugly face of yours!" Torune barked out with finality, and Imara began to tear up at hearing the insult her father would always use against her.

"You don't even know me," Imara pleaded weakly, to which Ron finally intervened.

"That's enough!" he said, stepping into Torune's face. Torune bowed up at the taller man.

"What? Am I hurting your ugly girlfriend's feeli—" Torune's words were choked back as soon as Ron seized him by the throat and lifted him off the ground.

"If you can give me one good reason I shouldn't kill you right now, I might just let you go," Ron said, and Torune could only choke and sputter as he squirmed helplessly in the air. "Yeah, I didn't think so," Ron said as he put the other hand on Torune's throat and began to squeeze harder and harder. Torune tried to summon some of his chi, but this just made Ron choke him harder until he lost his focus. As soon as Torune's face started to turn purple, Imara stepped up.

"Ron, he gets the point," she said. For an agonizing moment, Ron hesitated. And then, he dropped Torune. The rebellious hot head gasped for air as he scrambled away from Ron. "Consider that your one and only warning!" Ron commanded. Torune was too busy gasping for air to argue, and even the stronger of Torune's clique seemed shaken by what they witnessed. "Anyone else? You especially look like you're going to be particularly problematic," Ron said as he squared up to one of Torune's stronger built friends. The man wisely backed away. Ron seemed satisfied. "Good."

Sensing a break in the tensity, one of the female members of the Sanctorum felt it safe to step forward. "Leave it at that. We have our orders," she said, diverting Ron and Imara's attention to her.

"Orders?" Ron asked, though it was noticed that his voice was lowered to a less confrontational tone. The Grand Priest spoke up.

"Koroa is talking about the training assignments. You all will partner up and train for scenarios in which you will face the Elemental Conversion you have the weakest affinity for. I've been told that you specialize in more than one of the Elemental Conversions," the Grand Priest explained, to which Ron pondered.

"Oh, yeah. I've always liked Earth Conversion the most, but Dad taught me what he knew of Fire Conversion and I learned a little bit of Lightning Conversion from mom," Ron said truthfully. The extent of what he showed Imara as it concerned his use of Lightning chi was a teleportation technique, but she suspected he might have known a little more about the Elemental Conversion than he let on. Especially around Raj.

The Grand Priest nodded. "Koroa here has mastered all five of the Basic Elemental Conversions, as well as received as much combat training as you have. She'll take good care of your progress," the Grand Priest said, and with that, he dismissed everyone in the Sanctorum.

"And what will my training consist of?" Imara asked. At this point, Imara and her family swore they saw a ghost of a smile appear on the prince's face as the Grand Priest turned to her.

"Be honored, Priestess Gimura, for you shall be allowed to train alongside the prince himself," the Grand Priest said, and Imara's eyes twinkled for just a little bit.

"Royal training, for someone like me?" she asked, seriously wondering what she did to deserve it.

"Of course. As will Marshal Jotomatu and Consul Nokosi once they both have equal mastery of the basic Elemental Conversions," the Grand Priest explained.

It took a moment for Imara to register that Nokosi might have been Koroa's family name, but that was mostly because she was stumped at the titles the Grand Priest used. "Did you refer to Ron as . . ." She started, before Azuro interjected. "That's right. I have big plans for my reign. Some of which involve ending our ancestral war with the Changelings once and for all. To do that, some changes need to be made. Including that the heads of my Imperial Court be more versatile than the one that came before." Azuro said.

"And it starts with me. Here and now."

Three Hours Later:
Azuro's Training Court

Azuro and the Grand Priest waited; Imara was taking her sweet time getting ready for the first training. He wondered what all the Empress was explaining to Imara, and why it couldn't wait until after training. Even Imara's mother had returned before her; Azuro was starting to get impatient. "Your majesty, do try to relax," the Grand Priest attempted. Azuro didn't even acknowledge him as he began to do some warm-up exercises. He had just barely finished his one-hundredth push-up when he heard a footstep behind him. Azuro jumped to his feet, knowing that Imara had shown up.

"So, where did they put your scimitar, Imara?" Penelope asked. Azuro was about to chastise Imara for being late, until he turned around and got a full view of Imara in her purple tights and her black tank top. That moment of shock was just enough for him lose his train of thought momentarily as Imara answered.

"They locked it in a safe at first, and then brought it to my suite. I didn't even know why there was just a random safe in my bedroom, until they told me this. At least they knew better than to touch it with their hands," Imara said, happy that they didn't make the same mistake that General Tensai made.

"Imara, you're late," Azuro said, hoping his tone didn't betray his previous distraction.

"Oh, I'm sorry. The Empress insisted on sharing some things with me. I told her that you were waiting," Imara explained. Azuro realized looking at her lips while they were curled into that smile one gives to hopefully disarm and earn sympathy was a poor idea, so he forced himself to look at her eyes as he said his next words.

"Be that as it may. Training begins now. Show me what all you know," Azuro said, as he assumed his stance. Imara was about to set her weapon down, when Azuro stopped her. "What are you doing? I said show me all you know," he said, but Imara simply looked at her scimitar.

"But . . . you're not armed . . ." she started.

"It doesn't matter. But if you must, we'll start with unarmed combat training first," he relented, not having the patience to convince her otherwise.

"Thank you, your majesty," Imara said, as she laid down her weapon, and stepped into the clearing.

Azuro and Imara both took their starting stances; the Grand Priest could almost see the differences between the two fighters before they even began. "Begin!" the Grand Priest said, and the two young fighters did just that.

Penelope felt a bit of pride swell up at watching Imara sparring with the Crown Prince. The Gimura matriarch was the only one present in the outdoor sparring court that could tell just how far Imara had come from the wild haymakers and the flailing kicks of her first battle. In fact, Imara looked as though she put in the necessary effort to truly hone and perfect what little Raj had taught his wife and daughter.

But that was just it. Penelope knew on some level that Raj ensured that she and Imara were taught only what they needed to be useful on the battlefield and to not be victimized should they be separated from the main Force, but not much more. Everything else that Imara learned was self-taught, and it showed against the Crown Prince. So far, Azuro had mostly allowed Imara to remain on the offensive, and only really dodged or diverted her fierce strikes.

However, what Imara had learned in experience from battle she lacked in finesse. Each and every time she overcommitted to a haymaker or a kick that would have knocked out a militiaman, Azuro put her on her back. Whether it was a well-timed redirection of momentum or sweeping her remaining leg from under her in the case of a kick, Azuro was always on point with his precision and technique. He did not need to move quickly or match Imara's ferocity, his calm diversions and dodges more than saw him through during his defensive play.

But now, as soon as Imara got back up from being floored for the fifth and final time, it was the Crown Prince's turn to go on the offensive. His style was best described as "graceful brutality." As he practically danced around Imara''s defenses, he didn't "throw" punches or palm strikes so much as he allowed them to flow when they may and become solid when they reached his target. Imara was always just missing Azuro each time she made an attempt at a counterattack, and kicks above the shin were punished with a swift sweep as soon as her knee had been chambered.

The Grand Priest didn't even need to say it; Azuro used Wind chi to summon his sword right about the time the five-minute round would have been over. Imara looked to the Grand Priest, then Penelope, and then for her weapon. After a moment, Imara simply summoned the cursed weapon and got into a ready stance. "Ah, the sorceress makes her appearance," Azuro said, unable to hide the softening of his voice as his eyes accidentally gravitated to Imara's legs that he knew just glistened and rippled under her tights from the workout. He cleared his throat, as he forced his eyes to look at her face. "What are you waiting for?" Azuro called out, brasher and more impatiently than he intended.

As soon as the Grand Priest gave the signal, Imara closed the distance. Azuro gasped as he just barely dodged Imara's first attack and found himself taken off his feet for the first time when she kicked him in the chest while he was still recovering. He backtracked, the change in pacing and urgency from the prince earning a small smile of pride from Penelope as she watched.

Imara had firmly seized control of the combat dance, and Azuro knew it. The direct approach and ferocity that caused her to be predictable in hand-to-hand training now made her unpredictable during armed training. Imara's slashes and footwork were quite basic; Azuro had learned most of the moves she used before he was ever even allowed to use a live weapon. But it was clear that this was her main method of battle. There was not a sign of trepidation or hesitation in her movements, and Azuro at times forgot that this was merely a sparring session.

What's more it seemed almost like he was . . . distracted a bit before he got serious again.

"Time!" the Grand Priest called. Even Azuro was breathing heavily, but Imara had dropped to her knees in exhaustion. He was about to say something, until he laid eyes on Imara's legs once again, especially as she sat in a relaxed seiza position. Despite his best efforts, his gaze lingered on her curves far more than was proper or polite, and he only really noticed he was staring when Imara looked up at him with a softened expression.

Azuro thought fast. "It's rare that those who master sorcery enough to wield a Troll Scimitar or a Reaper Scythe are able to also hold their own in physical combat. For most who have the magical prowess to do so, physical combat is deemed to be beneath them. But not you, which puts you a cut above even expert sorcerers," Azuro complemented, and Imara's face couldn't help but turn red given the way he had stared at her just a moment before. He looked away for a moment as she stood; he couldn't risk staring at her legs again as they were moving and rippling.

"Just how many Elemental Conversions have you mastered?" the Grand Priest interjected, to which Imara stopped and thought.

"I honestly don't know. I just kind of practiced what I read about when I could."

The Grand Priest pondered for a moment. "Let's start with the fundamentals. The basic Elemental Conversions." The Grand Priest led. Imara looked to Azuro.

"Well, perhaps the Crown Prince has something to teach in this regard?" she asked sincerely, her lips curled into an innocent smile as she said this. Seeing those big pink lips smiling at him made Azuro's mind wander, but he quickly looked at her eyes to force himself to refocus.

"Hmph," Azuro said, as he summoned a wreath of Fire chi around his right fist; the same hand he had wielded his sword with. In the next moment, he summoned a swath of Water chi around his off-hand, and when he brought his hands together a ball of Wind chi was conjured and became the nucleus of the atomic model he generated with his power. The Water and Fire chi swirling in perfect balance was beautiful to behold, as Imara and Penelope both stared in awe at the demonstration of perfect chi manipulation.

Azuro dissipated the energy, before looking at Imara and Penelope with a confident, self-assured look. Azuro let a bit of his pride show upon seeing the impressed look on Imara's face. "It's not often one masters more than two basic Elemental Conversions. Some sorcerers spend their whole careers trying to master even just a third Conversion," he preened. He then looked at Imara. "If you're as talented as everyone says, let's see if you can use three Conversions in perfect tandem as I did," he challenged, and Imara appeared to become nervous as she looked to her mother for the answer.

"Imara, don't worry. Just show the prince what you can do," Penelope reassured, and Azuro's prideful look only set further.

"Okay. Well . . . here goes," Imara said, as she closed her eyes, raised her hands, and took a breath.

And when she let out her breath, five orbs coalesced above her head. All five Basic Elemental Conversions were accounted for. Earth, Wind, Water, Fire, and Lightning; each Conversion was represented in their purest form as balls of energy. Now allowing her mind to wander, she began to rhythmically and smoothly dance with the five levitating orbs as they moved about her. Penelope giggled silently at the wide-eyed stare the Crown Prince and the Grand Priest were giving her daughter as she beautifully and perfectly performed the drills she had witnessed her father and Atto lead the Gimura Force in during training.

Imara cupped her hands together, bringing the five orbs together in her palms and mixing them perfectly before opening her eyes, signaling the end of her frenetic dance. She seemed to remember that she was in front of people as soon as those snake-like eyes opened, for her focus immediately wavered. As soon as she did, the compressed ball of energy seemed to involuntarily explode outward, knocking her onto her rear. Azuro and the Grand Priest, thankfully, got out of range the second the energy orb's lines became wavy.

"I'm sorry . . ." Imara apologized innocently. "I completely forgot I wasn't alone." She gave that sheepish smile again, and Azuro forced himself to look at her eyes yet again. The Grand Priest simply nodded.

"You kept all five elements perfectly balanced, for about as long as you focused. How? How did you balance them out as perfectly as you did?" he asked. Imara shrugged.

"Why does everyone ask that? If I could explain it, I'd happily teach everyone what I know," Imara said. If they could handle learning from me, that is, Imara added mentally, but realized the thought of her father's attitude had creeped back into her mind.

"I think I can put it into words . . ." Azuro began.

The Same Time as Azuro's Explanation:
The Sanctorum Training Grounds

"So, let's see if I have this right . . ." Ron said, having just finished listening to Koroa's breakdown of Elemental Conversions during the break in their sparring session. He seemed to be gaining energy as opposed to being tired out by talking and sparring at the same time. It had been a while since he had a worthy sparring partner, but here Koroa Tensai was.

"The basic Elemental Conversions of Natural chi all have interactions with one another, and they all balance out in the end?" he asked, and Koroa nodded.

"Yes, that's right," she said, and Ron continued.

"And most people are born with a proclivity toward one Elemental Conversion over all the others." Koroa once again affirmed it.

"Good to know you can listen and fight," she said, though unlike with Torune and his friends there wasn't a hint of sarcasm in her words. Ron was tempted to allow a prideful look to come across his face in front of the pretty warrior complementing him, but he didn't let himself get distracted.

"Now, if I'm not mistaken, the Basic Elements are Earth, Lightning, Fire, Wind, and Water. Now, Earth has an advantage over Fire and Lightning, but has a weakness to Wind and Water, correct?" Koroa simply smirked at this; of course, Ron would be most concerned about how his affinitive chi interacted with the other Conversions. However, she was keen to test how much he was listening.

"Yes, but what about the other Elements?" She led, and Ron followed.

"Well, Lightning is strong against Wind and Water, but as I just said it's weak to Earth and also weak to Fire." And of course, he was also concerned with the affinitive chi of his opponent, which was her at this moment. That'll be useful during combat assignments for sure, she thought.

"Anything else you learned?" she said allowed, to which Ron clearly had to think. Koroa was about to explain again when Ron seemed to remember.

"Oh, right. Water is strong against Fire and Earth, but weak to Lightning and Wind. Wind is strong against Water and Earth, but weak to Fire and Lightning. And finally, Fire is weak to Earth and Water, but strong against Wind and Lightning," Ron recounted the last Elemental Conversion with a chuckle; it was good to know his affinitive chi trumped Torune's affinitive chi in case he ever acted out of line again.

"That isn't all there is to it, you know. For example . . ." almost as soon as she had said this, she raised her hand. It possessed a glowing outline of Lightning chi, and Ron noticed his body also glowed for a second before he found himself being pulled toward his dark-skinned, blonde-haired sparring partner. She was pulling him into a very solid kick. But Ron was not about to get kicked by those solid, heavily muscled legs if he could help it. Summoning his chi, he curled up into a ball and materialized a stone coating around himself. Koroa just barely switched gears in time to jump out of the way, and the ball of conjured rock formed a crater on impact.

"Good reflexes there," Koroa complemented, her adrenaline coming down as she registered that this sparring session almost ended with her getting crushed. Ron hatched from the earthen egg he surrounded himself in.

"Oh, that was cheap!" he chastised, but Koroa just placed her hands on her curvy hips.

"You expect your opponent to fight fairly?" she asked with a snarky look on her face.

"A surprise attack proves nothing!" Ron complained. To which Koroa shrugged.

"In your case, it proves that you know full well that sometimes affinitive advantage isn't everything," she said, and Ron suddenly realized the point of the surprise attack. And with that realization came another question.

"But you shouldn't have been able to use the Lightning Pull or the Lightning Push on me at all. Even my dad couldn't do that," Ron pondered, to which Koroa simply smirked again.

"I doubt Atto tried hard enough. Pretty sure he taught you everything you know about Elemental Conversions, and from what I see that's not much," she taunted, to which Ron raised an eyebrow.

"Pretty sure you were on the defensive for most of the training."

It was both true and untrue; Ron was definitely a warrior before a sorcerer. Sure, he would occasionally muster up the basic energy blast or even conjure up a stone coating as he did during Koroa's surprise attack. But Ron much preferred to simply turn his arms and feet to stone in order to enhance his strikes or increase his overall strength.

"Hmph, I was holding back myself, you know." Koroa wasn't lying, but she wasn't about to completely admit that Ron had really gotten the better of her more than she'd have liked. As a Lightning Conversion user, Koroa was not slow in either physical or reflexive speed. Nor was she weak, and with her skill in combat her explosive physicality was put to great use. However, she simply did not hit as hard as Ron could, nor could she take as much punishment as he could. There were times where just one of Ron's punches counted for five of hers, but she compensated by ensuring that he only ever got one hit in exchange for every five or more she landed.

"I'll tell you who won't hold back real soon," Ron said, a dark look coming over his face. Koroa followed his line of sight, to see Torune and his friends approaching.

"Hey, Koroa, I see you started the training session without me," Torune hollered out, his friends not too far behind. Ron glowered at him, but this time there was no sign of backing down from the thuggish former successor.

"If you're done making out with your new boyfriend, we're ready to train," Torune's friend from earlier said, his voice exactly what one would expect from an uneducated heckler.

"How rude can you guys get?" Koroa demanded, not backing down from the solidly built male in front of her. Ron's fist tensed up, but he was ignored.

"How rude of us? You're the one who started training without us. We all know why you and him went off alone," Torune's friend taunted.

"Sounds more like you're jealous, Leo," Koroa taunted. Leo simply got closer to the dark-skinned blond.

"Of what? Getting with you?" he said defensively, his tone becoming more aggressive.

"My man needs to be able to comprehend the words I use, thank you very much. Or at least have finished high school," Koroa continued, to which Leo took offense at the insult to his intelligence. It didn't help that Ron laughed at this.

"What, you think just cause you got a degree from some university, that you're better than me?" Torune and his friends pulled up behind Leo, attempting to intimidate the one female present with their numbers.

And now Ron stepped in. "Real tough. A bunch of grown men ganging up on a woman," he said, earning the attention of Torune's gang.

"You're talking a little big there, tough guy. The Grand Priest isn't here, so you plan to go one on seven? You don't expect the little lady there to help you, do you?" Torune challenged, as Leo and the other five members of their clique also squared up and got ready for a fight.

At this, Ron pressed the C-Ring he had been given by the Empress, and in short order fifty armed guards teleported onto the training grounds and assumed a ready position. "Your math is a little off there, buddy," Ron said, smirking as Leo and Torune both backed up and rejoined their friends. Koroa, for her part, remembered something Ron said earlier.

"Ron, when did you . . ." she asked in awe, realizing who these fifty troops must have been.

"You didn't think Imara was only concerned about my well-being alone, did you?" Ron said, drinking in the horrified reactions of the lower-class roughnecks as the Gimura Force was reunited and still just as loyal as ever.

"Now, Priestess Gimura may be the leader of the Sanctorum, but I'm the one who decides who stays. And right now, I'm not convinced that I want any of you seven in any platoon of mine," he said, and almost as if the order was explicitly given, the former Gimura Force followed the implicit order to surround and threaten Torune's clique.

Koroa's face seemed to soften at the sight of this, but pointedly she hesitated in her decision. "Hey, come on. We were just playing around. We just wanted to test how brave you were, that's all," Leo nervously said, any previous pressure in his tone all but suppressed in the face of the consequences he was about to face. Ron laughed.

"Yeah, you tested my courage. And since you all of a sudden like tests, here's yours," Ron said, as he signaled to the rest of the Gimura Force. "You are gonna stand and fight me. Alone," Ron said, cracking his knuckles in preparation. Leo's eyes bugged out at the prospect of fighting the experienced warrior without backup.

"For what? I've got no reason to fight you," Leo simpered, and the snarky look on Koroa's face just spelled out what she thought of Leo's sudden loss of courage now that he would be fighting Ron in single combat.

"Yes, you do," Ron said, as the Gimura Force promptly forced Torune and his gang back to the audience stands. "You're going to fight me here and now, one on one. If you refuse, or if you so much as cheat or try to get up to your little street rat tricks, you and your little friends are gone from the Sanctorum for good," Ron challenged, and the nervousness on Leo's face said it all.

"Look, I'm sorry for the way—"

Ron held up his hand. "Save it. You don't mean it. Don't insult me like that again. You have five seconds to get on the black top before the Gimura Force carts you out of here," Ron said forcefully, and began to retract the digits on his raised hand as he counted down. "Four. Three. Two!" Leo finally stepped onto the black top.

"Okay, fine," Leo relented, releasing this was the point of no return as he took his fighting stance. Ron did his best to not laugh at the crude, basic stance in front of him as he looked to Koroa to give his command.

"Set the clock, then ring the bell."

Five Minutes Later:

Azuro's Training Court

"

. . . Understand, now?" Azuro had wrapped up his rather lengthy summary of the Basic Elemental Conversions and their Evolutions. Imara nodded.

"I do. And no wonder Dad failed sorcery school twice. Wow," she said, thinking back to just how many conventional Elemental Evolutions there were, let alone how many abstract Evolutions could be achieved by adding Physical or Spiritual chi to the mix. Her mood plummeted when she thought about the fact that she, alone in her family, had the talent she did. Azuro simply smirked.

"Trust me, sorcery school isn't for the mediocre or the untalented. Taj and Raj both had the same opportunity; it's nobody else but Raj's fault that he failed twice." Azuro attempted to reassure, but hearing her uncle mentioned reminded her of a certain memory. Now was as good a time as any to ask.

"In your explanation, you mentioned that one can find out their Elemental Proclivity in a number of ways. The easiest of which is the chi litmus test?" She led, and Azuro followed.

"Of course." She turned to the Grand Priest.

"Did my dad and uncle ever take that test?" To this, the Grand Priest stopped and thought.

"They would have had to in order to be admitted into Sorcery School," he said.

"Did you ever keep the results?" she said, and the Grand Priest shook his head.

"No, but I'm sure your uncle still has those records." Imara was about to ask more questions, when one of the maidservants walked onto the scene.

"Your highness!" she called out. Azuro stood his full height, as though he were taller than his height of five-nine. And right now, one believed he was the tallest man in the world based on the way he carried himself.

"Speak. What news do you bring?" he asked regally. The maidservant simply handed him a missive, and it was signed in the Empress's handwriting. "Ah, I see," Azuro said, as he opened it. After a few seconds of reading, Azuro looked up.

"Of course, she would," Azuro said, as he turned to Imara and the Grand Priest.

The Sanctorum
Training Grounds

The Grand Priest teleported Azuro and Imara directly to Ron and Koroa's location, just in time to witness Ron knock Leo down yet again. Leo just barely rolled out of the way the finishing stomp, but Ron threw a side kick that took Leo right on his chin and sent the hapless man to his back yet again. This time Leo found it quite difficult to get back up, but Ron helped him to his feet by lifting him off the ground by his neck. For a good forty-five seconds, Ron wailed on the exhausted miscreant with his free hand and his knees. Leo's suppressed grunts of pain only hardened Ron's resolve, as he knew that Leo was never going to give him the satisfaction of letting him hear a scream of agony.

At least, not voluntarily. "Hmph. So, you won't give up, eh?" he said, as he knocked Leo to the ground. Leo feebly struggled to get back up, but Ron brought all of his weight down with all the force he could muster right on Leo's arm. The resultant snap was drowned out by Leo's bloodcurdling scream, and even Azuro cringed in sympathy pain for the defeated crony.

"Enough!" Imara called out, getting Ron's attention.

"Imara? When did you get here?" As he asked this, he noticed that the Grand Priest and Azuro were also present. He looked to Koroa, who herself seemed to just now notice the new arrivals as well.

"We teleported in as soon as we got this missive from the Empress. Where's Torune?" Imara explained, and her question took the rest of Torune's clique off guard. However, the man in question stepped up.

"A missive from the Empress, eh?" he said, as he took from Imara and read it.

After a few seconds, Torune went pale at the news. "Oh, my god. Really?!" Torune exclaimed in incredulity. "The Empress is actually doing this?" At this point, Leo had managed to pull himself back to his feet; Imara cringed when she saw just how many places Ron managed to shatter his arm with one stomp. "What did I miss?" Leo asked. To which Torune glowered at his snake-eyed rival. "The Empress actually wants me to bring this ugly trollop along with me to retrieve the last Troll Scimitar." Torune said, earning a low growl of anger from Ron.

"The last Troll Scimitar?" Koroa said.

"Yes," the Grand Priest interjected before Ron could step up. "Our scouts on the front lines reported that the last scimitar was likely in the possession of the rogue Priestess Grendella Al Singh." Imara tilted her head at hearing her mother's maiden name. She had assumed that the rest of Penelope's family remained in America.

"Al Singh?" she asked, but the question would never be answered.

"Why do I even need Imara, anyway? I can easily execute Grendella on my own." At this, Ron was quicker on the draw.

"This is a retrieval mission, you damned fool. And last I checked, Imara was the only one here who can even touch a Troll Scimitar without losing her mind," Ron said, and Torune pointedly did not back down where the rest of his clique did. However, Azuro thought fast before the tension could spike anew.

"I am sure that, if taking orders from Imara is going to be a problem, then I'm sure Torune would be more than happy to accept orders from Zume instead." Azuro looked and sounded like his mother right about here, and Torune couldn't help but make the comparison as he was mentioned.

"Ugh, fine. Alright. I suppose I'll partner with Imara," Torune relented. The Crown Prince simply narrowed his eyes at the older, taller man.

"You are to follow her orders, Torune," Azuro commanded.

"I don't think I need to tell you what happens if Priestess Gimura doesn't return, for any reason. But I will tell you what happens to your friends, should that happen." Azuro glared at Leo, who was still nursing his broken arm. Leo looked as though he was ready to cry tears of fear at what he knew was coming.

"Don't worry about Torune following orders. He knows how things are supposed to work," Leo said, and the worried, yet angered stares the rest of his clique shot him told Torune all he needed to know. Seemingly satisfied, Azuro moved on.

"According to our scouts, Grendella should be returning to her hideout in four days. More importantly, the Changelings are sending a little welcoming party of their own around that time. You two are to get there before that point, and hopefully swipe the scimitar before the rogue priestess returns," Azuro said, and Imara nodded.

"I understand. I'll be sure to set out tomorrow at dawn," she said.

"Oh, and Imara?" the Grand Priest started, getting her attention. "The Empress has ordered that you choose a different weapon for this assignment. We can't risk this rogue gaining control of another Troll Scimitar," he explained.

"So, this assignment is basically going to be Imara shouting orders at me from the background while I do most of the work?" Torune challenged, to which the Grand Priest was quick to respond.

"If Priestess Gimura commands it, then that's what shall be done. Now, Zume . . ." at the mention of his name, the sorcerer by that name teleported onto the scene, ". . . escort these two to the armory, so that they can choose their weapons." The Grand Priest's order given, Zume looked at Imara and Torune both and wordlessly motioned for them to follow him.

Three Minutes Later:
The Sanctorum Armory

Even the weapons storage facility was expansive, with so many places to hide if one didn't want to be seen. It honestly made Imara uneasy and wary that anyone could be watching at any moment. Torune, for his part, was clearly unafraid as the three of them walked in silence. Zume held up his hand, indicating for them both to stop, before pointing to Imara.

"What's he—?" Torune started, before Imara stepped forward and summoned some Natural chi into her left hand and Physical chi into her right. Zume grinned in approval, as he conjured some Spirit chi in his right hand and Physical chi into his left. Upon doing so, both placed their hands into each of the four keylocks on the door. The proper chi requirements met, the door slid open with a loud creak. Torune simply tilted his head in confusion. "How did you—?" to which Imara simply smiled that sheepish smile of hers. Torune was likely not even listening to her anymore, but he didn't want to admit that he was no longer looking at her eyes anymore as she spoke.

"Well, he needed the door opened, and those four keylocks indicated they needed certain chi to activate them," she said with as soft and gentle a tone as she could muster. Torune, however, didn't quite get it.

"How?!" Torune said, far more aggressively than he needed to. Imara's face softened as she heard the edge in his tone, but it was the fierce, angered look in Zume's green eyes that told Torune everything he needed to know. Specifically, Torune became rather intimidated by Zume stepping forward and intervening on Imara's behalf.

"I simply read the intent behind his eyes, that's all," Imara said, hoping that she could diffuse the situation.

"You could stomach looking at this animal's eyes?" he asked incredulously.

Imara's own eyes were rather off-putting, so she really didn't quite see why one would have a problem looking at Zume's own crossed, lazy emerald eyes. They were focused now, which really highlighted how captivating they actually were. Really, Zume was quite handsome if not for his crossed eyes and his creepy stare. Zume's hard, angered stare at Torune continued for another few seconds before he wordlessly motioned for Imara to join him. As she walked into the armory, Torune attempted to follow. That is, until Zume jumped in front of him and raised a hand, Spirit chi blazing into a ball of potent energy ready to blast his adversary away. Torune simply backed away, and when he was past the door Zume closed it.

Imara breathed a sigh of relief. "Thank you. I was tired of holding my tongue," she said when Zume rejoined her. He simply smiled at her. "So, is it true? Are you actually mute?" she asked gently, to which Zume nodded. His eyes were crossed again, and Imara started to realize that it was a sign that he was relaxing and allowing his guard to drop. "Don't tell anybody . . ." Imara couldn't help but giggle at the irony of her own statement, and Zume himself simply gave her a snarky, yet playful look. ". . . but I honestly wonder what Torune's problem with me is. He's only known me for less than three days and he hates me as much as . . ." Imara became saddened as she almost spoke aloud the truth she had become very aware of since the day she saved her father. "I just wish I had a solution to their problem with me."

They had made it to a sealed vault as Imara said this, and almost as though to answer her question Zume held out his hand and fired an energy blast. The two-ton door in front of them was instantly vaporized without a trace, and Imara's eyes went wide at what she witnessed in said vault.

For sitting in front of the two young sorcerers were the Five Tools of the Elemental Sages, complete with the Talisman of King Oberon. Imara couldn't help but examine each weapon in turn; they were exactly as they were described in every single book she read concerning high-level sorcery and mysticism. She honestly didn't know which weapon to choose and didn't know how much time she had to make her choice.

That is, until Zume handed her the Talisman of King Oberon. "Wait, you're just giving me all of them?" Imara asked with incredulity. Zume nodded. "But what will the Empress—" Zume placed a gentle hand on her lips, shushing her entirely. Her faced involuntarily reddened, but once she was quiet, he activated the talisman, retracting the weapons into the artifact. He then guided Imara's other hand to completely cover the talisman, and she felt her inner energy spike and then meld with the Talisman of King Oberon. She wondered if this kind of power was what the first Elven King felt when he wielded these weapons.

"The Empress has much faith in me?" Zume nodded, but then also indicated himself as well. "But . . . you just met me. How can you know the Empress is right or wrong about me?" she continued, to which Zume just grinned at her. Imara didn't know why, but something in his eyes just told her that she was right to interpret his unspoken body language and expressions the way she did. "Thank you, Zume. For all you've done," she said, as he began to lead her back to the entrance. However, as soon as Zume passed by her, she swore she heard someone speak.

"You are very welcome, Imara."

Noon the Next Day:
The Outskirts of Gimurdina, Almurkarzia

Imara and Torune had both ridden in silence for the past two hours. Torune pointedly kept turning his head away from facing Imara or otherwise averting his eyes, not wanting to stare at her legs every time she crossed or uncrossed them. Any and all attempts at small talk on her part was met with either glares or terse responses from Torune.

Despite the tension between the two, Imara couldn't help but wonder how long it'd take for her to get used to being chauffeured by a royal attendant. In fact, she wondered how long it'd take for her to get used to palace life in general. She couldn't remember the last time Raj had fed his entire force as well as she was fed last night; it was no wonder weight and fitness was such a concern among the royals and the nobles. However, she felt almost guilty in indulging herself as she did, whilst the rest of her family were unable to join her.

"Gimurdina . . . is this where you're from, Gimura?" Torune asked, and for once he took his eyes off of Imara's legs long enough to look her in the eye. Imara's thoughts were interrupted, and she looked up to see that they were indeed approaching the city named after her clan.

"It is. And it's supposedly where the scouts last tracked our target," she said, perhaps a little too jovially as she savored the moments where Torune wasn't outwardly angry with her. "Uncle Taj has an Oracle Statue that will help us better locate Grendella's exact movements. We should make it there before she gets to the lair." At this, Torune scoffed.

"Ha! We're just going to sneak in and take the scimitar without giving this rogue what for?!" he taunted, and Imara simply blinked.

"Why would we risk ourselves in an unnecessary battle when it's as simple as walking in discreetly and simply finding it with chi sensing?" she asked, hoping Torune would see logic. However, the flame-headed former successor was simply not having it.

"You can retrieve the Troll Scimitar your way if you want, but I'm waiting for Grendella and bringing her back to the Sanctorum dead. If you don't want the glory of bringing down a traitor to the Imperial Court and just want to 'play it safe' like a coward, then be my guest," he said, and Imara wondered if he quite understood just what they were facing.

"Torune, Grendella is a rogue priestess. As in, her skill with sorcery is such that she achieved that rank in the first place. Even if she were just a mid-level sorceress, isn't this enough reason to be on our toes?" she reasoned, but Torune didn't even so much as consider her argument. "Look, you're a coward, as I suspected. But just watch me bring Grendella down without so much as breaking a sweat."

Imara was honestly happy that they had made it to their destination; she didn't know how long she wanted to deal with Torune's boasting. "Good, we're here," she said, as she was quick to exit the vehicle. Torune followed, but pointedly remained standing behind her at all times. Imara's face might have been jarring, but even Torune had to admit that she had inherited the rest of her body from her mother. Imara's luscious black hair and her curvy, hourglass figure was quite a sight to behold from behind, especially as she walked in those tights of hers. Torune found his eyes involuntarily lingering on her once she turned around, and this honestly angered him so much more than he would ever admit.

First, you humiliate me in Imperial Court. Then you have that damned retard threaten me, and now you disrespect me further with your very figure?! Oh, how easy it'd be, right now, to destroy you! Torune thought, his eyes flashing with real and unbridled anger as he found his fist shaking with anger at his rival unintentionally seducing him without her knowledge. No, this gladhanding, simpering wench knows full well what she's doing. Torune ranted mentally, his eyes doing their best to tear themselves away from Imara's figure as she continued to walk. He remained silent; he was not about to let her bait him into action yet again.

"Oh, good, it's where I remembered it being," Imara finally said.

"And what would you have done if this sta—ah . . ." Torune's thoughts stopped cold when Imara bent down to place her fingers in the eyeholes of the Oracle Statue in question. His eyes had gone wide at the sight of her bending at the waist, and for the briefest of moments his hatred of her was forgotten before it redoubled in his mind. Now I know she's doing it on purpose. If she thinks she can just seduce me into falling in line . . . Torune thought, until even that was interrupted when he laid his eyes on Imara again.

"Hmmm . . . interesting," Imara said as her eyes glowed from using the Sight of Oracles. Torune barely registered her words. "Her 'hideout' isn't so hidden. She has just cast a Camouflage Illusion on her house," she said as she stood back up.

"Wasn't your mom's maiden name Al Singh, Imara?" he asked, and the weakened, tiny voice practically announced his innermost feelings right about now. Imara, for her part, was just happy that there wasn't an edge to his tone for once.

"It was. And I remember how often Mom took my brothers and me to Grendella's house. So, this location works out perfectly," Imara said as she stood up and turned around. "Are you okay?"

She asked, seeing the priceless look on Torune's face. He had not caught himself in time, but he shook his head clear upon seeing Imara's face. "Never mind that!" And there it was again; Torune's anger and bluster had returned with a vengeance. "Let's just go get this damned scimitar already!" And this time, Torune made sure to walk ahead of Imara.

"Where are you going, exactly?" she asked after she took a few steps. Torune stopped cold and turned around to see Imara staring at him in a snarky manner, her hands placed on her curvy hips. Torune was fighting a losing battle not to stare at her body again. "Grendella's house is that way. Just follow me, okay?" she said, and turned her back yet again.

Torune took a breath, before following along. He wondered how long he'd have to look at Imara's tempting backside.

Thirty Minutes Later

Thirty minutes of walking, and there was still no sign of Grendella's hideout. "I thought you knew the way! Where are we going?! There's nothing but grasslands as far as I can see!" Torune barked out, to which Imara turned to look at him. She was using the Sight of Oracles, so her snake-like eyes were blank. She perhaps looked better like this, but Torune didn't want to let himself get distracted again. This, however, meant he noticed the snarky, chastising look on her face. She signaled above her, and Torune's eyes went wide.

"Tracker Hawks!?" he said, seeing the two birds circling above them before taking off in the direction just in front of them. Torune prepared some chi in his fingertips.

"Don't bother," Imara said, uncharacteristically serious as she did. Torune couldn't help but take notice, as she sounded like a war general now more than ever. "She already knows we're here," she said, looking directly in front of her. The rogue priestess knew that there was no use hiding, and so she dispelled the Camouflage Illusion.

Torune's jaw dropped for just a moment before he caught himself. He had to hand it to the Al Singhs, they could produce the prettiest, most enticing women he'd ever laid eyes on. One look at the soft olive skin and the hourglass figure Grendella shared with Penelope and Imara was all that was needed to tell she was related to his hated rivals.

"I was under the impression that the Grand Priest would be showing up. I even got all dolled up for the occasion." Grendella's voice was exactly what one would expect from a vain, pampered sorceress, and Torune narrowed his eyes at this. "Imara? Is that you?" Grendella asked, now seeing that the young woman adorned in the most luxurious royal breastplate and black silk tights she'd ever seen was in fact the daughter of her cousin. "My, how you've grown. The years in exile has turned you into a beautiful young woman." Torune wondered if Grendella was looking at Imara's face as she said this, but then she turned her attention to the former successor. "I'm sure the Mujin boy here has more than noticed." Torune became incensed at this; he was a man of twenty-five and being referred to as a mere "boy" just hit all the wrong nerves.

"I'm not a kid, you old crone!" he said, as Imara felt his chi raise and then change into Elemental Conversions. "If you want backup, just call on me," Torune said as he jumped out of range.

"Ah, a family affair is it?" Grendella asked, as Imara activated King Oberon's Talisman and summoned a sword and shield set; the additional weapon she was allowed to choose yesterday.

"Gi-Gi, I don't wish to fight you. The Empress has ordered us to retrieve the Troll Scimitar you possess, but that's it. Just hand it over, and I'll argue for your amnesty." Torune clenched his fists at Imara's words, while Grendella actually seemed to consider this offer.

"Perhaps someday, you, Penny, and I could catch up on our own terms. But today . . ." as Grendella spoke, she conjured up some Spirit energy, and began to weave and meld it before pressing both hands onto the ground. And when she did, the ground beneath them shook and heaved before an ethereal, person-sized urn was summoned.

"Wait a minute . . ." Imara said, realizing what Grendella had just done. More importantly, she also realized that the height of the ethereal urn was exactly seven-five; there was only one person she knew of that could have been contained within that summoned urn.

This was then confirmed by the contents of the urn poured out reconstituted into none other than a familiar towering, hulking form. "Ser-Sergeant Goering?!" Imara said, incredulous at just who Grendella had summoned using the Impure Resurrection technique. At this, the revived thrall of that name simply looked to Imara.

"Gimura, daughter . . ." he droned mindlessly, and Sergeant Goering's intelligence being this heavily suppressed perturbed Imara more than the fact that Grendella was able to summon him with Impure Resurrection.

"Goering, do what you shall to the Mujin boy. Leave Imara to me," Grendella ordered.

As soon as the revived Goering heard this the towering, big man launched himself at Torune with surprising speed. He just barely dodged a breaking punch from Goering; Torune was happy he wasn't the tree that Goering just shattered into splinters. Torune conjured his dual tonfa and was quick to imbue them with Fire chi as he leapt in to engage the massive thrall. With perfect agility, Torune danced and dodged around the colossus's powerful swings while delivering solid blows of his own with his melee weapons. Torune never stayed in one place long enough to be hit or grabbed in response, and always seemed to duck and dodge out of Goering's reach just in time. Finally, after dodging one last stomping kick from the towering colossus, Torune managed to get some distance and unleash a Fire Shroud from his eyes, causing the undead Goering to burst into flames.

Meanwhile, Grendella had willed eight more thralls into existence with her Impure Resurrection technique and had sicced them all on Imara. However, this was exactly what the younger sorceress was hoping for, as now this meant she could put her sword and shield to good use as she engaged all eight of them. She alternated between well-placed slashes with the sword and solid, crushing presses with the shield to keep her eight undead opponents at bay, but eventually she found herself surrounded in any case. Imara noticed something rather odd about Grendella's tactics, but she didn't have time to think about this as she jumped over two of the thralls who tried to catch her off guard. She took them both out with a spinning split kick, snapping their necks on contact. The other thralls backed away, apprehensive of how to attack. Not that they had the chance; Imara promptly used her sword as a guide for the energy beams she fired at her remaining six opponents.

As soon as the last thrall had fallen, and Torune had rejoined Imara in facing the rogue priestess, Imara began to speak. "I'll say it once again. Hand us the scimitar, and I'll request your amnesty," she said, and upon seeing the same snarky look from the beautiful older sorceress Torune had no doubt about which side of the family Imara got her seductive capabilities from.

"Always so presumptuous, just like your mother," Grendella taunted, and almost as soon as she said this did the undead Sergeant Goering jump from the flames Torune thought he engulfed him in.

And hear, Imara noticed the oddity yet again, as Goering pointedly aimed his destructive smash mostly at Torune. The shockwave of his double-handed ground pound was corralled away from Imara and aimed entirely at Torune. Not that it hit him, for Torune jumped away in time. Imara realized she had also dodged on pure experience and instinct alone, but it wasn't lost on her that she wouldn't have needed to dodge that attack at all.

As soon as she landed on her feet, she took a massive inhale, right as five of the eight thralls managed to recover and regenerate enough to be functional combatants again. And as soon as they were in one piece, Imara unleashed her Ice Breath. Grendella's summonings were all frozen solid, right as Torune finished supercharging himself with Explosion chi. Imara swore he was moving as fast as any Lightning Dasher when he dashed forward and rammed his fist into Goering's gut.

It was called Explosion Fist for a reason, for that's just what happened when Torune's fist sunk into the undead outlaw sergeant's belly. The resultant explosion engulfed not only Goering, but the other frozen thralls as well.

"Hmph. Is that it?" Torune preened, before the smoke cleared away. For what it was worth, the other thralls caught in the peripheral explosion were indeed vaporized by Torune's handiwork.

"You'll find that he's just a little harder to kill now that he's been revived." Goering's stomach wound was already starting to regenerate, and Torune promptly regained his distance as quickly as he got into melee range.

"Well? Any bright ideas, priestess?" Even now, Torune couldn't resist showing his contempt for Imara's authority. But here his sarcasm would backfire.

"Actually, I think I have a way to dispel the bonds of the Impure Resurrection. If you can just distract him." Torune's face fell at hearing this, and Imara began to build up some Spirit chi in her weapons. However, Imara's plan was ultimately unneeded.

Sergeant Goering's eyes went blank, as his arms tightened up and turned to steel. Grendella's eyebrow involuntarily rose as she sensed the unexpected influx of chi. Goering's chi, asserting itself at this moment. "What . . .?" she asked in surprise.

"Have you forgotten that I am Sergeant Shan Goering? I do not fight for your pampered tyrants, and I will never serve another selfish noble!" Sergeant Goering's intellect had returned. The undead pallor of his skin and the reddish vein-like tron lines were still present, but Grendella felt her control over Goering slipping.

"Well, that's disconcerting," she said, as she was forced to dispel the Impure Resurrection before the undead colossus could fully regain control over himself. Sergeant Goering's body turned to ash and dissipated, right in time for Grendella to see a beam of Nuclear Energy closing in on her.

She just barely jumped over it, and she used her airtime to summon a protective barrier around herself as she landed and began to flee to her house. "Gi-Gi! Stop!" Imara called out and began to chase after her relative. But Grendella had already made it back to her house and activated the Lockdown Procedure. Imara blinked. "Torune, I know a Teleportation Technique that can bypass even chi dampening force-fields. If you just give me a mom—"

Imara's mouth fell open in shock when she saw five comets of Explosion chi sail past her head and at Grendella's house. Once they surrounded the house, Torune clenched his fist and the orbs centered into the guarded house. The resultant explosion erased Grendella's house right out of the existing realm.

"Hey! Come on now!" Imara said in disbelief.

One Hour Later:
The Vehicle Ride to the Gimura Residence

"**W**ell, at least we got what we came for . . ." Imara said as she cleaned the soot from the hilt of the Troll Scimitar they managed to retrieve from the wreckage. There was no sign of Grendella; even her chi had dissipated almost as soon as Torune ignited his Five Star Explosion technique.

"At least? I killed a rogue priestess, in case you missed it," Torune blustered, to which Imara simply rolled her eyes.

"We can't say for sure that we killed her, due to your little stunt," she reminded, to which Torune simply blustered more.

"It'd be really out of the ordinary if she survived that attack."

Imara simply crossed her legs, and now Torune was certain she did this to taunt and tease him. "You're lucky the scimitar survived the explosion pretty much unharmed. What would we have told the Grand Priest if it had been destroyed?" she asked. Torune pointedly hesitated, and a look of concern came over the hotheaded imperial relative. However, that look of concern was soon replaced with belligerence.

"I'd tell him that it's the fault of his successor for being an ugly failure!" Imara's pupils constricted at hearing what her father would always call her.

Before the hurt could set into her mind, a voice from outside cut into the conversation. "Ugly failure, eh?" Now it was Torune's eyes that dilated in fear, as it was clear his voice carried enough to allow someone outside of the vehicle to hear.

Imara opened the door, and she sheepishly looked at her uncle. Raj's younger brother stared a hole through Torune's soul, and the imperial relative nervously grinned in hopes of disarming who he just knew was a protective uncle.

"So glad you could make it Imara. How's Raj?" The way he said it suggested that he perhaps already knew, but Imara's mood sinking more than spelled it out without a word needing to be said. "Come in. We've much to talk about for the next two days," he said, placing a comforting hand on Imara's shoulder as he helped her out of the car.

"Uncle Taj? Despite what you heard, Torune is in fact a subordinate of mine and is a guest until we return to the Imperial Palace. I'm sure he won't make you regret your hospitality," Imara said genuinely, but Torune couldn't help but feel as though there was an edge of danger as Taj glowered at Imara's jealous subordinate. He turned to his manservants.

"Prepare the guest room for Imara's friend."

Underground Hideout, Unknown Location

Grendella had just barely managed to teleport to safety before the orbs of the Five Star Explosion could detonate. She swallowed hard, as she prepared to face . . . them. She slowly placed her hand into the handprint lock on the door; it was a relatively quick action, but for Grendella it was the slowest move she ever made in her life as she knew what would happen as soon as her chi was read and identified.

"Grendella Al Singh," an automated voice sounded. Her eyes dilated when she saw the hologram of a brownish-skinned man in his early sixties. The golden silk cloak really emphasized the old man's slumped, ambling, almost feral posture as he stared lecherously at the beautiful sorceress. Grendella felt her skin crawl. "I see you've returned," he said, to which Grendella nodded.

"I wish to enter, Mr. Goodvibe," she said in a quaking voice, hoping that this wasn't a mistake.

The massive door creaked open, revealing the Round Table. Grendella thought the name was odd, since the "table" that the heads of the Goodvibe Syndicate sat at was more like an escalating arch than a table. In fact, Grendella felt more like she was walking into an Imperial Reception Hall than a secret underground hideout. And seated at the highest, centermost point was the man who had appeared in the hologram.

Grendella felt her mind ease a bit when another voice called out. It belonged to one of the men sitting directly beneath Goodvibe's throne; the one to his left was unmistakable. "Your highness, I—" the one she addressed stood up, and Grendella felt her throat seize up involuntarily. The man sitting to the left of Goodvibe tilted his head.

"Synturo, what are you—" the man addressed held up his hand.

"Save it, Goodvibe." As Synturo said it, Grendella noticed that a tracker hawk perched itself on the former Crown Prince's arm. One of the tracker hawks that Grendella made use of.

"The Mujin Dynasty takes care of its own," he said with finality. There was no denying that Synturo was the eldest son of Kato Mujin and Malkia Anmin. He was quite tall and possessed entrancing amber yellow eyes, while being as well built as his maternal grandfather and uncles and possessing the light brown skin of his mother. What was more, his voice was smooth, rich, very powerful and as beautiful as he himself was. All of this, in addition to his regal and imperious demeanor would give one every reason to believe he was already an Emperor who deserved nothing less than the utmost of respect.

"We will return," he said simply, as he motioned for his followers to form a ring around Grendella. Synturo himself completed the ring and teleported his inner circle out of the main meeting room.

Mujin Dynasty Meeting Room

As soon as Synturo's followers rematerialized in their sector of the Syndicate Hideout, all of them backed away and took their seats. "Sit," Synturo ordered, and Grendella did. Her legs shook as she did, but Synturo seemed almost as though he was in a good mood as he stroked the tracker hawk on his shoulder. "Well done," he said, taking Grendella by surprise.

"Sire?" she started in a tiny voice. Synturo smirked at the look of shock on the older priestess's face.

"I must commend you for drawing out Mom's little contingency plan. And surviving a fight with one who could wield any of the Accursed Armaments or tame the Talisman of King Oberon and all that it contains without ill effect. In one skirmish, you also managed to reveal each and every single one of her weaknesses in the process," he said, but Grendella was still uncertain.

"I . . . My house was destroyed, as were most of my weapons and talismans. And I lost the Troll Scimitar," she informed, to which Synturo simply shrugged.

"It doesn't matter; we will simply have the house rebuilt and more armaments procured for you. It's hardly a fair trade, however, for the invaluable information you have given this Court." Synturo stood. "We will be recruiting the Gimura sorceress soon enough. Mom's contingency is full of holes that are easily exploited. For now, you other four continue to fulfill your orders." The other four members of the Mujin Dynasty bowed, as they teleported out of the meeting room. "And Grendella?" he said, having noticeably made his way toward the older priestess as he placed a reassuring arm on her shoulder. The sorceress felt her guard immediately drop.

"Your idea to try and recruit the Mansa Army was a sound one. Try to bring it to fruition," he said gently. However, Grendella was still not certain about one thing.

"But what of Imara? How are we to bring her to our side?" she asked, to which Synturo looked her in the eye.

"Once Qilin and Goodvibe fulfill their ends of the bargain, we will enact that plan in due time," Synturo said, as he dismissed Grendella. As soon as she teleported out of the hideout, Synturo teleported back to the main room.

Syndicate War Room

Synturo had barely reappeared when Goodvibe started in on him. "Well?" the old man asked, to which Synturo simply folded his arms. Goodvibe ambled lazily over to the much younger former prince. Even if he stood his full six feet, he'd have been visibly shorter than Synturo. So, it went without saying that Synturo positively towered over the old man when he was in his slumped, almost feral posture. That didn't mean Synturo took him lightly as he professionally responded.

"Grendella is still useful to my plans. Even in failure, she has revealed new ways to achieve our goals." Goodvibe's face contorted with anger.

"You mean you didn't punish that old crone for her failure!?" Goodvibe exclaimed, and now he stood his full height, his golden cloak no longer skimming the floor as he did. Synturo narrowed his amber eyes.

"She didn't fail, and I'd appreciate it if you didn't speak of my subjects that way, Warwick," he firmly, yet calmly responded. Goodvibe's pupils constricted at hearing his first name used; to say he was incensed was an understatement.

"In case you don't remember, I am the only reason you are even able to still pretend that you are still royalty. If my forces hadn't sheltered you, you'd be dead in a ravine like the commoner your father was." There was exactly one grain of truth to that statement, and both men knew it.

"Warwick, the five you see sitting beneath my throne were those who remained loyal to my father, and then to me. They aren't exactly the rank and file, nor will I treat them as such," Syn said, to which Goodvibe laughed.

"I don't need this conversation. From what I've seen, there's really only one good use left for Grendella. If you aren't going to make her useful, I certainly can." He lecherously grinned at the thought of his uses for the experienced sorceress, but now Synturo's composure cracked.

"Yes, Warwick, you do; you want to conversate with me right about now. Understand that your Syndicate needs the Mujin Dynasty as much as we need the Syndicate's resources. And I will not tolerate you speaking of my subjects in that manner again." Goodvibe considered challenging the younger, bigger man.

"Don't forget, that the Chimera Clan also stands to benefit from its alliance with the Goodvibe Syndicate." A deep voice with just a hint of an East Asian accent sounded, diverting the attention to the leader of the Chimera Clan. Qilin was currently masked, so the only clues to his Asiatic ancestry were his eyes and the skin tone of his muscled arms. The iron mask, sleeveless grandmaster gi, and the crested helmet symbolizing his leadership position were the only indicators that the Chimera Clan were supposed to be ninja primarily. Otherwise, Qilin was just as tall as Synturo, with muscles easily at least one full size bigger than the former Crown Prince; Goodvibe couldn't help but wonder how he could be so stealthy as he was.

Synturo, for what it was worth, stood his ground as Qilin continued. "Our interests align, so we must stand together and put our differences aside for the time being. Failures and set-backs are unavoidable, but they should not become common." The warning in Qilin's voice wasn't lost on Synturo; he raised his eyebrow at the veiled threat the Changeling Grandmaster had managed to deliver without spelling it out completely. However, Qilin then made a motion, and now both younger, bigger men turned to the old man in front of them. Goodvibe smirked at this little show of unity. "However, this is an alliance; do not think for one moment that you can do unto us as you please. We need your resources, yes, but make no mistake, Warwick. We all know it is not merely Empress Anmin and Emperor Idate you are worried about."

And now the petulant Goodvibe lost his cocky, taunting demeanor, for just a moment. "Let's be adults here. After all, until she is dead at my feet, your interests align with mine by default." It was true, but the point was made.

And the matter at hand was clear.

8:00 AM Two Days Later:
The Elven Sanctorum Temple Grounds, Ron's Training Room

Ron had just barely finished his warm-ups when he heard footfalls stop just a little distance away. He took a breath, before turning around. "Ah, Koroa. And . . . Zume . . ." Ron had to admit that Zume's crossed-eyed, blank stare and the way he lolled his head to the side when he wasn't engaged in the world around him did give him the creeps at times. However, he also knew that Zume had a mental disability and honestly felt bad when he let himself feel this way toward a handicapped person.

"So, what brings you two here?" he asked awkwardly, pointedly not looking at Zume as he said this. Koroa simply put a hand on her hip.

"Zume has something to give you," she said, as she directed Ron to look at the mute Sanctorum member yet again. Zume's eyes focused, and he looked almost normal for a moment as he handed him a talisman with the Gimura Force logo on it.

"What's this?" he asked. And now Koroa allowed him to look back at her.

"It's something the Empress's scientists have been working on since Imara was delivered to the Imperial Court. The Gimura Force will be joining the war effort soon, so it's better that you all have access to Spectral Energy as soon as possible." As Koroa was explaining, Ron began to examine the seal.

"So, this is what the eggheads at the prison were talking about when they said the Gimura Family seal would be recycled well," Ron said to himself.

"Speaking of, Imara should be back soon. The prince made a special seal for her to add to King Oberon's Talisman." At Koroa's words, Ron's eyebrows raised.

"An addition to King Oberon's Talisman? Isn't Imara carrying enough power within that thing as is?" Zume's eyes refocused, as Koroa spoke what he thought.

"Prince Azuro did say he'd take good care of his next Grand Priest. And, anyway, Azuro wants her to report for some training as soon as she gets back," Koroa informed.

"Not just her either," Azuro's voice sounded, getting everyone's attention. "It's about time I inspected the Gimura Force in its entirety. Especially if it's going to be fighting on mother's battlefields." Azuro looked around. "Should Imara and Torune be ba—"

The doors to the training room opened as Azuro was speaking. "Ron, I'm back and Uncle Taj said—" Imara froze when she saw Ron, Koroa, Zume, and Azuro already present in Ron's training room. "Oh, hi everybody. I'm back," Imara nervously said as she realized she interrupted something.

"Good," Azuro said as he looked at Imara. "Where's Torune?" he asked, and it took Imara a moment to remember.

"Oh yeah, he said something about going to visit his friends." Azuro took a breath.

"I told you to tell him to report to me as soon as you got back," Azuro said, and try as he might, he couldn't muster any anger toward the snake-eyed priestess.

"I tried to tell him, but he wouldn't listen. He kept saying that I'm not Grand Priestess yet, so I shouldn't order him around." Ron felt his arms tighten, but he took a breath. Zume's eyes refocused upon hearing that, and his head no longer lulled lazily to the side. Koroa didn't need to be a mind reader to realize how these two felt about Torune and his friends.

"Hmph. You four," Azuro turned to the four non-royals, "be ready when I return. I have some orders to deliver to Torune and his squad," Azuro said, and the angry edge to his voice wasn't lost on the non-royals.

8:15 AM:
Torune's Suite

"She really said that?" Leo laughed, hearing Torune's viewpoint on the previous assignment he and Imara had to complete.

"On everything I love, she did. That ugly wench was in awe as I led her right to the rogue priestess's house. Unlike those little boys that Raj recruited, Imara was finally in the presence of a real man," Torune preened as he said those words. Perhaps in his mind, he was telling a true story.

"Oh, but it gets better from there, especially after we actually get to the rogue priestess. The cowardly crone didn't even want to fight us herself; she could feel my chi and the look of fear in her eyes were delicious. She summoned up as many undead peons as she could. There must have been about a hundred of them, each and every one armed with assault rifles and great swords. But not one of them could save their rogue summoner from my Explosion Fist or my Nuclear Evolution." Torune's words left his lips as though they were the truth. In fairness, he was right to say his Explosion Fist took out multiple opponents. And perhaps that was why his friends didn't question it.

"What happened next?" another of Torune's clique asked, and the boastful Mujin was only too happy to oblige.

"Exactly what you'd think. The rogue priestess tried to run away like the coward she was. But I put a stop to that and blew her up with my Five Star Explosion," Torune said, gathering miniature versions of the technique on his fingertips. "Imara practically fell out of her clothes when I saved the day. I bet she'd even beg me to take her if she wasn't so damned ugly." That earned a laugh from the rest of Torune's clique.

For all of a few seconds. "Is that what happened." The laughter halted abruptly when Azuro's voice sounded. Torune had no idea what all the Crown Prince heard, but the look on Azuro's face indicated that he heard enough.

"Yeah, of course it was," Torune said, though his voice shook. Azuro narrowed his eyes. "Look, your precious priestess came back alive and unhurt. I did my job," he said, and perhaps the Crown Prince was starting to lose patience with his standoffish cousin.

"Yes. And I have another for you. For your whole squad," he said, as he looked over all of them. Counting Torune and Leo, there were seven of them in all.

"All of us?" one of the smaller, leaner squad members asked.

"Yes, all of you. And all of you are to come back alive. Is that clear, Torune?" Torune's eyes widened just a bit, before he relented.

"And just what is the mission?" he asked, hoping to change the subject.

"Reports from our scouts indicate that the Mansa Army has been sighted in Osai. Specifically, near the capital district of that territory. We believe they will strike soon," the prince informed, to which Leo tilted his head.

"And you want us to link up with the County Chief's forces and intercept them? Isn't this a job for the Gimura Force?" Azuro shook his head.

"They will be training with me in the use of their new Spectral Talismans until they are ready to join the war effort. You have until 10:00 to get ready. Torune, get to work." Azuro turned and was about to leave when his cousin raised his voice.

"Is that little training exercise really for improvement, or do you just want to get closer to that ugly girlfriend of yours?" Torune taunted, earning snickers from his clique. Azuro did not so much as turn around.

"At least try to sound like you aren't jealous, Torune."

Azuro walked out of the main room, leaving a dumbstruck Torune to process what the Crown Prince just said.

8:30 AM:
The Imperial Training Room

Imara never thought she'd actually be happy during a moment like this. Though she and her brothers lined up as they normally would for Raj's sound off, they didn't even have to bring their weapons. Rather, they simply presented their seals. "It's odd how familiar this chi feels," Hassan noted, as he swore the chi was very familiar indeed. However, logic dictated that his thought on the matter couldn't be the case.

"Yeah . . . Where did you get these, exactly?" Adam asked. Azuro took a moment to think before answering.

"They were made after you were released from prison." Jericho wasn't satisfied with that answer.

"How, exactly? There's a lot of power in these." Azuro shook his head.

"The scientists said that information is classified, even to me. It is a question for my mother." Zume's eyes refocused as he heard this, the snarky look on his face saying it all as he heard Azuro's words. "In any case, what is important is that everyone equips their seals so that training can begin. Now!"

Imara noticed how quick the Crown Prince was to change the subject, but she stepped forward. "I'll go first," she nervously said, forgetting that Raj wasn't around to lambast her for showing initiative. Azuro merely nodded.

"Good. Set the example for your Force to follow," he encouraged, and now Imara found her confidence as she equipped her seal and closed her eyes to concentrate.

Azuro steeled himself and summoned up all his focus to watch Imara's frenetic, yet somehow well-ordered kata as she gave a demonstration of her Spectral chi usage. As she did for the Basic Elemental Conversions, she took a breath. And when she exhaled, two energy orbs of Spectral chi were produced. However, this time, the orbs took form. The form of a hominid male and female, and though they possessed an undead pallor it was clear these two thralls were not passed souls at all. And as soon as they took shape, Imara began her kata.

The Gimura Force and the Crown Prince all watched as Imara demonstrated that she had complete and total control over her summoned thralls, for they mimicked her war dance perfectly when she wanted them to and fulfilled their designated parts without Imara even having to give the command. Once it was over, Imara dissipated the Impure Summoning, and her thralls disappeared. She opened her eyes. Ah, so it does work like that, Imara thought.

"An Impure Summoning, and decently powerful thralls at that. A rather strong example of what I expect to eventually see from the rest of the reformed Gimura Force. Where did you learn this from?" Azuro's questioning of Imara's talent, for once, was one she could answer easily.

"I figured it out while Torune and I were retrieving the last Troll Scimitar," she explained, and only too late did she realize how oversimplified and easy did she make that sound.

"In the time it took you to fulfill the retrieval of the unclaimed scimitar, you figured out how to perfectly use Impure Summoning?" Azuro said, raising an eyebrow inquisitively. Imara smiled sheepishly.

"Well, I did have help from Gi-Gi when she used it to summon Sergeant Goering from the dead. And I just went from there," she said. Azuro seemed to ponder what Imara said, before turning to the rest of the Gimura Force.

"Demonstrations! Now! Imara is the standard you all need to meet!" The Crown Prince's orders were swift, deliberate, and clear.

11:00 AM:
The Highway, Torune's Convoy

The convoy driver cursed her unlucky stars that she ended up being Torune's chauffeur, but she was happy that the innuendos and passes had stopped after an hour. Mostly because now the conversation turned to different women and she was no longer the center of attention.

"Let's be honest though, Torune. You can't deny Imara's not too bad looking herself, if she closed her eyes. She's right there with Koroa, in fact," Leo said, earning approving concurrences from the rest of his friends.

"Yeah, and she expects me to buy that little sob story about how her daddy hated her 'ugly' looks. This is while trying to seduce me into obeying her orders," Torune said with a laugh.

"That sounds just like something Koroa would do. She has to know everyone is looking at her legs. She wants attention, just like Imara does." At this, the rest of the group laughed.

"You're right Shamir, they both know what they look like. Koroa and Imara both know what they have. And they're just like all the other women back at the village," another of Torune's friends said.

"It's probably why Imara smiles like she does when she's acting like a tease," yet another said.

The chauffeur was tempted to roll up the window, but she didn't do so out of fear that attention would come back to her. "One day, maybe I'll give her exactly what she's looking for. She wants approval, I know one way she can earn it," Torune said. The chauffeur stifled her gag reflex, as the conversation only got more abhorrent and perverted from there.

She wondered how she'd managed to endure the next two hours, but that was how long it took to finally get to the Osai County Hall. "We're here," the chauffeur said, and her skin crawled when the group of young men set their eyes on her.

"Good," Torune said, pushing past her as he got out of the vehicle.

"This goes well, you can celebrate with us, sweet-cheeks," Leo said with a lecherous grin. Shamir, however, gave her some gold coins.

"In the meantime, get yourself something nice. We got some outlaws to handle."

Osai County Hall, War Room

Torune and his clique entered the room, and all turned to bow to the cousin of the Crown Prince. Torune couldn't resist the chance to preen; it was times like this that he was happy his late uncle did manage to catch the attention of Empress Malkia. Everyone except for the County Chief knew their place as they saluted Torune and then all six of his inner circle.

The County Chief, however, did no such thing and it was noticed. "Torune Mujin, I see the Crown Prince was serious about sending some heavy firepower." The chief took out his clipboard. "Leoju Xuan," he said, accounted for Leo, and marked.

Torune took a breath of exasperation. "Xenju—" the County Chief didn't even acknowledge Torune using his first name as he continued to check the roster.

"Shamir Roquena," and Shamir was now accounted for. "Jomo Otunga," he said, saw the man of that name, and marked on his clip board. "Jotaro Otunga." Both Otunga brothers accounted for, the county chief continued his roll call, and Torune was growing more impatient. "Sekai Edris." Sekai's name was called, and he was then accounted for.

"Ghinjo Gatake—" Torune finally had enough.

"We're all here! Are you satisfied?!" he impatiently called out. The County Chief of Osai simply nodded.

"Yes. The Crown Prince will be happy to know you all made it," he said, as he teleported his clipboard away. "As you know, the Mansa Army has been sighted in this area and—" Torune interrupted.

"We're handling this now, Xenju. Tell your troops that the prince's cousin is on the job now."

"Master Nokosi, you can't possibly—" an advisor spoke up, and Torune fired a blast of energy past her head. She immediately froze as she was, her mouth agape from shock now as opposed to being interrupted. All went silent from the shock of Torune's action, and when no one spoke up Torune continued.

"As I was saying, I'm on the job now, and General Mansa and his clan are mine. My squad and I will bring them back to the Imperial Palace, dead. The rest of you, meet the underlings head on, and overwhelm them as quickly as you can. I want no interference during my fight with the Mansa clan. Is that understood?"

Chief Nokosi spoke up. "Torune, with all due respect . . ." At this, Torune glowered at the County Chief. He was undeterred.

"The Mansa Army cannot be fought with conventional tactics. Our manpower advantage means nothing against diversionary tactics and guerilla warfare." Now Torune teleported in front of the County Chief.

"You have a problem following orders, Xenju?" The Chief now stood his full six-four as he rose from his seat to meet Torune's aggression. His fist clenched, as Torune summoned up some Explosion chi in his hands.

However, Chief Nokosi relented just a bit when he saw Leo, then Sekai, then the Otunga brothers, then Ghinjo, and finally Shamir pull up behind Torune, clearly anticipating a fight. "Think about what you are doing, Torune. The Mansa Army isn't like any other rebel force. They should be treated as we would the Gimura Force." Hearing the clan name of his hated rival caused the energy gathered around Torune's fists to change to Nuclear chi. He pointed one of said fists in Chief Nokosi's face.

"And I wish you'd recognize who the hell you're talking to. I'm Torune Mujin; my squad and I are worth more than FIVE Gimura Forces! And when we win, I'll be talking to my cousin about removing you from your prefecture since you love questioning your superiors." The County Chief took a step back, clearly seeing there was no arguing at this point.

"If that is the case, we shall go along with your plan," the County Chief finally relented, as he stood down. Satisfied, Torune turned to the rest of the gathered Advisors and Officers present. "Get the troops ready! We'll meet the Mansa Army when they get here."

Midnight:
Osai Outskirts

A young man and a young woman bearing the Mansa Crest watched over the entire city. "Esau, I thought you told me this city would be a challenge," the pale skinned, copper-haired woman said. The younger, bigger male simply folded his arms.

"It's odd that they'd use a clearly inferior position even though they know we're coming. Also odd that they'd change so abruptly, too . . ." He pondered for a moment, before making a decision. "Let's go. Ranga, you can tell Dad we might need to change tactics in response."

One Week Later

Imara's heart raced; no matter how fast she ran those cold, dead eyes glowered down at her. Raj's yellow eyes followed her, no matter what.

"Damn you, Imara! You'd leave your father to suffer? While you enjoy the lap of luxury! Leading my armies?! Enjoying the fame and power that my genes granted you?! You truly are the ugliest of failures!" Raj's words sounded pained, and it soon became clear why.

His eyes, up until now, loomed over her as though he were the Grim Reaper himself. But now, his eyes were surrounded by Raj's abused, battered face and attached to his broken, crucified body. He was being tortured, but Imara couldn't make out any discerning features in his tormentors. All five of the torturers took turns stabbing him with their spears; not a single one so much as nicked a vital organ or artery. Raj convulsed in agony every time.

"You turned your back on me!" Raj screamed. Imara couldn't move her eyelids or turn her head, so she had no choice but to look at the horrific scene in front of her. "Are you happy? Does seeing this make you feel good? Do you think I deserve this!?" Raj continued.

Just then, what appeared to be a scientist teleported onto the scene, right as the other torturers disappeared. Raj's words became desperate, and as the world flashed white, Imara could make out the faintest of pleas.

"Don't leave me here! Please!"

8:30 AM:

The Imperial Palace, Imara's Bedroom

Imara was jolted awake. She looked around, and saw she was not anywhere near the Gimurdina Prison Camp. She took a breath. "It's just a dream. Again," Imara told herself. "He's dead! Forget about him and move on!" she told herself, realizing that Raj's death was truly haunting her. She heard a knock on the door; when she looked at the clock a realization came over her.

Uh-oh, I'm probably late for training, she thought as she jumped out of bed. And moved to the door. "Coming!" she said as she answered the door. Of course, it'd be Prince Azuro, and he didn't look happy at all.

"Imara, you—" Azuro stopped dead in his tracks.

"Your highness . . . umm . . . I'm sorry I overslept. Training was just so rigorous and . . ." Azuro continued to stare. Imara smiled sheepishly.

"I won't make any more excuses. I'm sorry," she said. Azuro's eyes were unblinking.

"I'm . . . sure exceptions can be made." Imara noticed that any edge to his voice was softened as he spoke almost unconsciously. And it is here where she followed his line of sight and realized why he was staring.

She forgot that she hadn't gotten dressed and was now standing before the Crown Prince in nothing but her rather revealing black bra and underwear. Her breasts looked more like honeydew melons that were just barely covered by the black, lacy bra, and her developed backside filled out the underwear in such a way that the temptation was almost unbearable. Imara smiling sheepishly just drew attention to her lips, and Azuro couldn't rip his eyes away from her.

"Umm . . . I'm so sorry, if you'd give me a second," she said sheepishly. She had no idea that she had just given him a much better view as she turned around to get her clothes. He could no longer look at her off-putting eyes, and before he could let his mind wander too far, he forced himself to look away lest the movements of her backside hypnotize him.

You cannot afford to be distracted. You are the next Emperor; hold it together! Azuro mentally berated himself; he hadn't expected to let his physical passions get the better of him as it just did. "I'm sorry for being late, your highness," Imara said, and to the Crown Prince's relief she was now clothed fully. Azuro shook his head.

"Just don't let it happen again," he said, his voice betraying the lingering surprise of what he just witnessed. He turned his back.

"County Chief Nokosi sent a request for reinforcements. I was here to tell you that the training plan for today has been changed. The true test of the Gimura Force will be saving the Osai Prefecture from the siege," he said as professionally as he could. Imara blinked, before asking the pertinent question.

"What . . . What happened to Torune and his squad? Weren't they supposed to be handling this?"

Azuro turned back to Imara. "They were. But then . . ."

The Midnight Before:
Osai Border Observation Tower

"As expected . . ." one night watchman said, as once again there was no sign of the Mansa Army.

"It's Master Mujin's direct orders . . ." another night guard said exasperatedly as he did his best to fight the urge to fall asleep.

"It's clear these Mujin rats have no idea what they're doing. Sending us on wild goose chases like this . . ." the second night watchman said.

"County Chief Nokosi had the best idea to simply fortify the defenses and wait for their pincer attack," the first night watchman said.

"Of course, we're the poor schmucks who get stuck with the night watch. If an ambush were to happen, we're the first ones to get caught in it," the second guard lamented sadly, yet with a resignation that indicated he knew how true this was.

"Ugh, I need a raise," the first guard wished aloud.

"Hey, our two-year mark is coming up so, that's something to look forw—"

Almost as soon as the reassuring thought was shared did an arrow of light pierce the observation tower's glass, and tear right through the second guard's mouth as he spoke. The first guard, to his credit, managed to scramble to the alarm and press it before the second arrow shaved his head down to the nose.

7:00 AM:
An Osai Beachfront Resort

Leo and Torune were woken up by the sounds of civilians screaming. "What in the . . ." It wasn't the fact that they woke up in the lobby of the resort inn; they remembered the festivities of the previous night and how well each could hold their liquor (that is, never as well as one would think). What they didn't remember was the alarm being tested.

"Everyone calm down!" Leo said, he watched the civilians scramble and troops rush to their battle stations. "It's just a drill!" Leo attempted, the headache from his hangover being made even more pronounced from all of the noise.

"Leo, my orders were clear. Xenju and his troops weren't to sound that alarm unless it was actually important," Torune said.

And just how urgent this situation was soon made itself very clear, in the form of bullets being sprayed into the lobby. Leo and Torune jumped to cover and were just happy that they weren't among the panicking civilians mowed down in the gunfire. Just as soon as the fire died down did a squad of bandits burst into the ruined lobby. "Kill all the surviving men! Keep the surviving women alive for Lord Mansa!" The leader of the squad ordered as he and his twenty subordinates.

"Lord Mansa?!" Torune said, and the squad of bandits all searched for the source of the voice. And that was precious time they wasted, for in short order Torune fired off two beams of Nuclear chi from his hiding spot. He was on the mark and disintegrated two of the bandits instantly. Their location now revealed, Torune and Leo barely managed to separate and jump away from the retaliation fire as they summoned their weapons. Torune's dual tonfa and Leo's single assault rifle was almost comical in the face of the remaining eighteen better-armed, better-supplied outlaw troops.

Almost being the key word, for just as soon as Torune equipped his dual tonfa did his chi Conversion switch from Nuclear to Explosion, and he suddenly no longer feared the speed of a bullet. He jumped over the bullets fired at him and punched the ground directly in front of him when he landed. The resultant explosion did its job and blasted the area in front of him out of existence. The entire half of the resort directly in front the Mujin upstart was blown away, along with twelve of the remaining bandits.

The six survivors who had managed to avoid the blast screamed in panic, and that only increased Leo's resolve and accuracy as he picked them off from a distance with one shot to the head each. Leo let out a mocking laugh as he saw the remaining bodies hit the floor.

"Easy enough," Torune said as he dusted his clothes off. However, Leo growled indignantly. "But what the hell were Xenju's troops doing? They're not doing their damned jobs!" he said. "I thought they'd have rounded up the Mansa Army by now. Or at least get the general himself," Torune concurred, annoyed that he just had to defend himself.

"If it's me you're looking for . . ." a deep, brutish voice sounded from behind them. Torune and Leo both whirled around and got in their fighting stances.

But it was too little, too late.

Back to the Present Moment:
Gimura Force Convoy

Koroa seethed as she finished reading the letter; her father was quite thorough in the details of the situation. "That stupid asshole!" Koroa said, her anger unable to be suppressed. Jericho simply continued driving; he refused to have a chauffeur lest his vehicle operation skills degrade from disuse. It was also a good enough excuse for not chiming in and saying what he thought of Torune's tactics. More pertinently, what he thought of Koroa's father for even agreeing to use Torune's tactics in this instance.

For that was expressed by Ron. "Now, why couldn't we get this lucky during our bandit days?" Koroa glowered at Ron, while Zume tilted his head. Before Koroa could really lay into Ron, Imara chimed in.

"What Ron means is that Raj would have taken advantage of every single hole and weakness in the plan Torune forced your father and his troops to use. Especially the parts where Torune had said troops scatter and form search parties as opposed to shoring up the defenses." Even Imara was incredulous at how dumb Torune's tactics truly were. "Worse, he then left only a tiny part of their remaining manpower as perimeter guards. The Gimura Force under Dad would have snuck into this city and taken it before the alarm could even be raised," Imara continued.

And that would have been the base of operations for Dad's attempt at seizing the crown. she mentally added, as her thoughts wandered to the idea of her father actually completing his goal of becoming Emperor. She wondered what kind of ruler he'd make, but she also got the distinct impression she'd never be anywhere near an imperial title or even near the Imperial Palace if he had his way. Imara's eyes teared up at the thought of just how much Raj hated her.

Zume saw this and put a comforting hand on Imara's shoulder. Koroa might have comforted Imara as well, but she was far more concerned about her own father at the moment. "All isn't lost however, if Dad is able to send an SOS signal like this. When we get there, I'm going to rescue my father," Koroa declared. Jericho was almost tempted to take his eyes off the road, and while Zume stared at Koroa in shock.

"Koroa, the plan—" Imara attempted.

"Means nothing for me if they kill my clan! Do what you have to do, Imara, but my agenda is my clan," Koroa said. The force and finality with which she said this shut Imara right down. Zume looked at Ron, who on cue spoke up.

"Koroa, there's at least five hundred troops in the Mansa Army. They outnumber us ten to one, and this before we account for the general himself and his clan. We get the urgency of the situation, but charging in blindly has never solved . . . well, anything really," Ron explained. It seemed to work, but Koroa huffed in defiance. It was clear she had plans of her own, and she was sticking to them.

"If all else fails, we'll all go with you ourselves. Jerry can lead about as well as I can," Imara reassured. Jericho felt a twinge of pride as he heard that, but he couldn't help but be a little wary.

"Imara, the general and his clan are likely directly holding Chief Nokosi hostage as the troops take the city," he informed, to which Imara nodded.

"I know. And that's why I leave the liberation of the city to you, Adam, Hassan, and Ron. You four follow the plan. As for Koroa, you said your basic affinitive Conversion is Lightning, didn't you?" Imara said. Koroa tilted her head.

"Yes, but what does—" Imara touched King Oberon's Talisman, and when she did she summoned the Lightning Needle. The weapon appeared on the floor of the convoy vehicle; Jericho wished he wasn't driving so that he could look upon one the Tools of the Elemental Sages.

"I know you aren't used to handling swords, but in this instance, I think you can make an exception." Koroa simply stared at the legendary weapon; she had only read about it in textbooks. But what she read about it, unfortunately, wasn't too promising.

"Pretty sure just holding that would constantly drain my chi," she said in a very dry tone.

"If your affinitive Conversion wasn't Lightning, then almost definitely. But I do think proficiency in your natural element really should allow one to work around that drawback," Imara explained, hoping it was good enough. For what it was worth, Koroa attempted to pick it up, and as soon as she touched the Lightning Needle did the thin, edged rapier glow with power.

"Oooh . . ." Zume's expression of awe sounded, his eyes now focused on the glowing weapon. However, Koroa let go of the weapon.

"I can't risk it. I need all of my chi to rescue my clan," she decided. Imara nodded in understanding, as she withdrew the weapons.

Koroa made a point; There was enough to worry about as it was.

Osai Capitol Building, County Chief Office

"Just wait until I get out of here!" Torune barked out, his voice permeating through the seal capsule tube he was held in. "When I do, I'm gonna melt you down and show that wench of yours how a real man handles things!" he threatened to his captors. Ranga simply scowled at this.

"When can we start absorbing his chi? He's annoying as all hell!" she asked.

General Mansa and Esau had both just finished sealing the rest of Torune's squad in the same suspended stasis capsules that he and Chief Nokosi were sealed in. "Ranga, we need to check their chi first before we just take it. Remember the last time we got chi we didn't know how to use?" he said, and Ranga cringed. "Besides, the readings indicate that there's a few Fire Conversion users among them," Esau said, to which Ranga's cringe set in further.

"Oh, of course," Ranga complained. General Mansa concurred.

"But that's why we have the Energy Distillation Capsules. Turn any incompatible chi into something more . . . useful to us," Mansa said as he turned to Esau. "So let's see these readings."

The outlaw general and his daughter checked the chi meter, and when they did their pupils constricted. "Nuclear Evolution? But . . . Who'd be so dumb as to teach this undisciplined street rat absolute mastery over Fire Conversion!?" Ranga exclaimed incredulously.

"HEY WENCH! I'm right here!" Torune said, taking offense to being referred to in this way by the outlaws and especially the female. General Mansa promptly kicked Torune's capsule over, rattling the young man as he pinballed around in suspension.

"You be as quiet as possible," he threatened, and the cocky upstart simply scoffed in defeat.

Esau had just barely finished calibrating the Energy Distillation when the chi meter began to sound off as though it were an alarm. Not that it was needed, because the new chi signatures were felt just a split second before the technological sensor sounded. "What . . . Is . . ." Esau couldn't believe what he felt and believed it even less once he saw the meter. "But . . . what would the Gimura Force even be doing here? This is rather far from their hideout," Ranga concurred when she saw the readings on the chi meter.

General Mansa, however, simply read the chi meter before an understanding look came over his face. "So, this is why Raj sent some imposter to lead his force after his failed coup; this is why he hid himself away for so long." He turned to his two children. "Esau, Ranga, this is as good a time as any to find out if we can dispel Impure Summonings. We'll meet Raj, and finally get ahold of his chi. And who knows; we might even get his daughter's chi to boot." Esau and Ranga both salivated at the idea of absorbing Imara's chi especially.

They wouldn't have to go far to meet the approaching Gimura Force.

Ten Minutes Later:
Inner City Osai

Koroa, Zume, and Imara made a direct course for the County Capitol; they were hoping that General Mansa hadn't detected them yet. So far, the plan was working beyond perfection. Imara had overestimated how many troops the Mansa Army employed; she remembered there being at least an extra platoon of outlaw soldiers the last time she had faced them. However, perhaps they all were excommunicated or else no longer part of the Mansa Army for whatever reason.

In any case, this definitely made the pincer attack so much easier to execute. And in the confusion, the three of them had managed to fulfill Koroa's wish to go search for her clan. "How long are they going to hold out?" Koroa asked, though it was clear it was not out of concern. Imara resisted the urge to preen.

"I'd say the Mansa Army should be surrendering after the fourth or fifth squad is defeated," Imara sardonically responded, earning a laugh from Zume. Koroa rolled her eyes.

"I don't want any distractions or unexpected visitors. Nor do I want any civilians caught in my crossfire," Koroa said, not really interested in humor right now.

"You're assuming much about the common citizen's courage, wouldn't you say?" a voice sounded. Koroa activated her chi.

"Who's there! Come out!" she yelled out; it was obvious to all present that Koroa was only too happy to turn her Lightning upon any who dared challenge her right now. The smile on her face when General Mansa and his two children appeared before the three Gimura Force members was only too telling.

"Oh, good. Just the one I wanted to see," Koroa said, as she extended the claw-blades on her gauntlets. "Where's my father? My clan?" she asked, her chi crackling as she was just one wrong answer away from fully cloaking herself in the Lightning Cloak. General Mansa, however, was not impressed in the least.

"He's still alive, for the moment. I should be asking why the daughter of Xenju Nokosi is working with bandits like the Gimuras." As he said this, Zume's eyes focused and his look became rather intense. Just in time for General Mansa to notice.

"Aren't you Lugato's younger brother? A Nderu on the side of the Gimura Force . . . Now I've seen it all," General Mansa said derisively. Zume simply narrowed his eyes at the implication, and even Imara summoned her weapon. The sight of one of the dreaded Troll Scimitars intrigued the Mansa Clan much more than it intimidated them, and the outlaw general especially did not break his bearing. Imara pointed her weapon at him.

"Consider this your one and only chance to surrender, Miro. If you do, I can promise amnesty for your entire army," Imara commanded professionally. The general simply tilted his head.

"Yeah . . . Go get your father. If Raj can beat me, then I might consider that little offer," the outlaw said, as though he were talking to a small child. Imara glared at the general's cavalier attitude, but Koroa simply ramped herself up with a Lightning Cloak.

"He's dead, you fool," Koroa said as she stepped up. Her patience was obviously worn.

The general couldn't have cared less, as he pointed the chi meter at the Gimura Force seals displayed on their combat gear.

"No, he's not. Bring him to me, unless you don't value your father's life."

And there it was. Before Imara or Zume could react, Koroa practically lunged over the ten feet of distance separating the two sides.

The sheer amount of force generated from Koroa and the general meeting each other was enough to send ripples through the air. Koroa's Lightning Cloak crackling simply added to the audible effect, but even with Koroa boosting her strength as she did the general still matched her and even pushed her back. The outlaw general stood roughly six-one compared to the five-five younger warrior, and right now he used it for all it was worth as he simply leaned his head just out of the range of Koroa's clawing swipes and kicks. Her claw-blades glowed with power, and the streaks were visible as she just barely missed the general's face each and every time.

Mansa finally caught Koroa's leg and threw her out of melee range. Esau and Ranga drew their pistols, though both wondered how effective they'd be against a Lightning Cloak user. Before they could find out that answer, however, Imara and Zume fired their respective energy beams. Imara used Spectral chi while Zume used Physical chi, but both beams were equally powerful as they blasted the firearms out of existence.

"She is not your only opponent," Imara challenged as she charged in, hoping she could distract General Mansa the same way she distracted Sergeant Goering that fateful day. Unfortunately, Imara only succeeded in getting Esau to bring his melee weapons to bear as he blocked her slash. Imara's snake-like pupils constricted when she noticed a very important detail. "Is . . . Is that . . ." Imara couldn't believe it, but the belt buckle on Esau's sash was no buckle at all. The sickly green glow that was emanating from said shiny "belt buckle" was unmistakably that of a Soul Reaper Jewel.

"It sure is," Esau confirmed as he dodged Imara's kick. He soon returned to Ranga's side, and Zume and Imara might have pressed the attack had General Mansa not used Wind Pull on the both of them and threw them at Koroa. Koroa stopped in her tracks, dodging under her allies who were just turned into projectiles. This diversion was enough to make her attack more predictable, allowing General Mansa to catch her clawed swipe.

"You're fast, I'll give you that." Koroa jumped up with all her force, bringing a thunderous knee to General Mansa's chin. To her surprise, the seasoned warrior looked more annoyed at being interrupted than damaged. "But you'll have to do better than that if you want to see your father again." Imara and Zume's eyes constricted when they realized what just happened. More importantly, Imara realized exactly why General Mansa didn't feel that attack.

"Koroa!" Imara called out. The dark-skinned blonde wasn't hearing anything else.

"Damn you!" Koroa called out, as she ramped up her chi and increased her Lightning Cloak to Stage Two. Zume became very worried, his eyes focused completely on Koroa's angered body language as her Lightning Cloak crackled fiercely. General Mansa simply smirked in the younger fighter's face, and she promptly drove her heel into his teeth.

Esau and Ranga both seemed to become optimistic, which only further set in the trepidation for Imara and Zume. Koroa charged at General Mansa, who seemed to dodge just enough of her attacks to keep her frustrated and angry, but even the attacks he allowed her to land did no damage to him. In fact, when she did "land" her attacks, he just laughed at her and made her even angrier.

Seeing exactly what General Mansa's strategy was, Imara looked to Zume. He nodded in understanding, as he teleported out of sight. Imara for her part waited for General Mansa to catch Koroa's kick and her through; seeing that happen, Imara put her lips together and unleashed a wave of Lightning Breath. The streaks of electricity nearly singed the general's hair as he was forced to dodge the unexpected attack. He was unable to dodge Koroa's flying kick, though he was definitely more surprised than damaged. Before Imara could follow up, her hand was grabbed by Ranga.

"Until your father shows up, I'm your opponent! And you're done for!" Ranga brought her daggers to bare, attempting to gut Imara then and there. If only Imara hadn't been quicker on the draw and teleported out of range. Ranga noted that this wasn't just any teleport, either. "Esau, she's probably using Hajitar's power!" Ranga said, as she activated her chi. Imara almost immediately noticed the change. More importantly, she remembered reading about just why Speed Conversion enabled the Masai Blitz Corps to be as deadly as it was.

And here, Ranga almost gave Imara a very deadly example as Hajitar's Shield was summoned right on time. The titanium daggers Ranga used snapped like twigs as they collided with the pink energy shield. Ranga backed away, looking at her broken weapons in shock. And those two seconds would have cost Ranga dearly had Esau not launched his chain at her, forcing her to divert her attack to dodge. Imara began to build up some chi in her mouth, and this was what General Mansa was waiting for.

"Perfect!" he said, teleporting out of the way of Koroa's attack and between Imara and his two children. "Yes. Give it all you've got!" he said, as Imara felt his chi change. She giggled, her voice echoing from the power she was gathering in her mouth.

"Oh, well, if you insist," she said, and General Mansa's pupils constricted when he figured out what the plan was. He had forgotten all about the mute warrior who had teleported just a short time ago. But Zume quickly made himself known again as soon as he reappeared.

And that reappearance saw Zume surprise Esau by swiping the Reaper Jewel in his belt. It took Esau a moment to realize what just happened, and by the time he did the silent sorcerer was out of range and teleported back to rejoin Imara and Koroa. "Koroa, power down!" Imara said, and the tiring Koroa had no problem doing so. Stage Two of the Lightning Cloak could only ever be sustained for a limited time, and she didn't realize how exhausted she was until she powered down.

"You . . . you fools!" Esau said, realizing exactly what was coming next.

"Now, Zume!" Imara yelled out, ignoring Esau's warning and literally crossing her fingers for luck.

To the Mansa Family's horror, Zume broke the Reaper Jewel on the ground.

At the Same Time:
Outer City Osai

"**Y**ou damned cowards!" a rather petite female outlaw screamed, recognizing the Gimura Force seal despite their imperial battle gear.

"Since when does Raj serve the Empress again!?" a male outlaw complained. Both were being tied up and tossed to the heap along with the rest of the complaining, surviving members of the Mansa Army. Out of the original 850 troops, Ron and Jericho both counted a hundred survivors in all.

"How disappointing," Adam said, as he watched the last of the Mansa Army either surrender or be defeated.

"I'm happy I never worked for General Mansa. Jeez . . ." Ron thought aloud. Despite there being more than 850 troops in the Mansa Army, the fifty-four members of the Gimura Force quickly and rather easily made short work of the comparatively uncouth outlaw rabble. Of all the things Ron and the Gimura sons could criticize the former County Chief for, the training and discipline he instilled in each and every member of his Force was not one of them. It really just showed how much better than most Raj truly was as a war leader.

"Does anybody else . . . feel that?" Jericho asked, and for once, it wasn't the strangely familiar Spectral aura that emanated from their new seals. However, the power was definitely Spectral in nature.

The gathered Gimura Force, as well as the remaining Mansa Soldiers, looked in abject horror as they then witnessed the sight of what was undeniably a Soul Reaper. "Is . . . is that?" One of the more experienced members of the Force asked.

"A Soul Reaper!?" a younger Force member gasped in panic. The other members stood in awe of the giant, grotesque being. Reapers wore the tell-tale cloaks in the mortal realm for the simple reason that their appearances alone were enough to trigger visceral reactions of disgust in those born to the living. At least this Reaper had dark brown hair to kind of offset his mummified, gaunt face. Otherwise, this thing looked as half-dead and zombified as any other Soul Reaper would on this side of the veil.

"Imara . . . We have to go save Imara!" one of the calmer members of the Gimura Force voiced what they were all thinking. And as soon as he did, the rest of the young men of the Force left their captives and immediately advanced to the location. They did not even hear Adam's order to proceed with caution. Nor did they see the Reaper begin to shrink. If anyone noticed either of these two things, Imara's safety took precedence over anything else.

Inner City Osai

Imara was happy the Reaper was not facing them when he appeared; his line of sight landed square on the one who originally wield his scythe. "Esau Mansa!" he rasped out, sending chills down the young outlaw's spine as he heard the giant-sized source of his powers speak. "And Maharajan Gimura. Fifty-seven of him?!" the Reaper said in a perplexed tone. Imara tilted her head at this.

"Yep, he's been in their too long," Koroa said, but Imara wasn't so certain. Zume simply gasped in shock as he heard those words, but before they could think anything more the unexpected happened. That is, what Imara had hoped for began to take effect. Almost as soon as the released Soul Reaper came to his senses, did General Mansa's chi activation make itself known as the Reaper's power began to trickle slowly toward him. Eventually, the Reaper began to also lose size and that was when things started to sink in for all on the battlefield.

"Augh?!" General Mansa's shout of pain was done in a way that most would say "What?" as he felt the trickle of power involuntarily flowing into him. However, soon the power of the Soul Reaper was no longer trickling over the outlaw general and soon rushed into him with the force of a fire hose. "AAUUGH!" This time, the scream of pain was done in a way that one would scream "HELP ME!" Mansa could no longer stand, as his body began to seize and then convulse as the Soul Reaper found itself being absorbed into the mortal outlaw. Imara stood over the general, his death throes getting more and more spastic.

"Figured as much. In any other case, being able to use the Energy Sink technique as proficiently as you can, would be considered among the greatest of advantages. But then, this isn't just any other case, now is it?" Imara said, her soft and demure voice perhaps more taunting with its seeming empathy than if she had outright insulted the outlaw general.

If Ranga was going to take offense to Imara's words, that hope was quickly dashed when the rest of the Gimura Force showed up at this moment. "Imara!" one of the young men called out. Before Ranga or Esau could react, ten of them teleported in front of Imara, forming a protective barrier in front of their snake-eyed leader. In short order, the rest of the Gimura Force had surrounded the Mansa Clan.

Esau looked to his father, and then to Ranga. "Where . . .?" Esau started, but likely knew the answer before the question was even formed. Zume's laugh said much more than any words could, but Ron answered anyway.

"The one hundred survivors have been captured and will be sent off for judgment." Esau and Ranga both seemed to not care for anything Ron had to say.

"Ranga, none of them will be fast enough to catch you, even with Stage Two of the Spectral Boost activated. You go to the men. I'll help our father." Ranga stared at her younger brother.

"Are you serious!? We both need to—" Esau cut her off.

"I'm not leaving him!" However, the voice to argue wasn't Ranga's this time.

"Son, join her. No need for both of you to perish alongside me," the general said. Imara stopped Koroa and Zume from making a move.

"Dad?" Esau said, unable to stop his eyes from tearing up.

"Esau, Ranga, you can always rebuild our army. You can always continue to fight for our cause. Even if Syn won't, remember to take care of yourselves, and take care of your mother. Esau, no matter what happens remember that you especially carry the pride of our clan with you everywhere you go." The general was struggling to keep the Reaper from taking him entirely, and it was a wonder the Soul Reaper didn't just straight up take him then and there.

"You . . . I . . ." Esau wanted to argue.

"Go!" the general commanded.

"Don't . . ." Imara ordered as soon as one member of the Gimura Force drew his firearm. "Let them go," she said solemnly. Even Koroa seemed to soften as the general now looked to the rest of them, just as soon as Esau and Ranga were out of sight. The general looked almost . . . happy. As if he was being relieved of all burdens at this moment.

Just as soon as that show of acceptance was seen did the outlaw general finally stop resisting. And the Soul Reaper feasted.

At the Same Time:
Mujin Dynasty War Room

Synturo watched the events in Osai unfold on the monitors, his eyes firmly fixed on Imara and Zume. The Gimura Force Seal attached to an imperial battle suit was something he never thought he'd see again, but there it was. More chillingly, a member of the Nderu Clan stood with said Gimura Force; Syn wondered what else his mother and younger brother were going to manage before Azuro was to officially ascend the throne.

"So, this is Grendella's talented niece. To wield a Troll Scimitar and lead a special operations force as efficiently as her father did . . ." Synturo pondered. He witnessed the Soul Reaper's release and the subsequent Spirit Drain of General Mansa. "Is she insane? She couldn't have known that was going to work out that way . . . Could she . . .?" he wondered, and then his suspicions were confirmed as he watched Imara order her troops to allow Esau and Ranga to retrieve their remaining troops and flee in defeat.

There was no longer any question in Synturo's mind. "Of course . . . She knew what would happen. And she wanted this to be seen.

It was the same with Grendella and how she acted like Torune blowing up her house wasn't part of the plan. She doesn't show 'mercy'; these are not acts of kindness or magnanimity. No, each and every person she sends back to me in failure is meant to be seen; she wants me to hear their stories." Synturo chuckled to himself. "And isn't it just the perfect timing that she sends this warning just in time for the State of the Territories meeting."

It took the former prince a moment to realize just what he said. His expression turned serious. "The State of the Territories meeting . . ." He had the monitors really focus on Imara from all angles. "She's as beautiful and sensuous as her Aunt Izuna was . . . Those snake-like eyes and that nose is perhaps off-putting to some, but to the Amphibian Tribes . . ." Malkia's elder son found his pupils constricting involuntarily as he remembered just who the current Amphibian King was.

"No . . . I can't let that happen!" Synturo decided as he teleported out of the Mujin Dynasty War Room.

Ten Minutes Later:
Goodvibe Syndicate
Meeting Room

Synturo never thought he'd see Goodvibe, of all people, with a panicked look on his face, but then he never thought he'd be telling him what he just did, either. "That can't be. It just can't! The Amphibian Tribes would be breaking an alliance with me if that were to happen!" Goodvibe seethed, now standing his full height. "They can't be that stupid. Surely, they'd know the consequences of defying my orders!" the old, petulant billionaire continued to rant.

Though Qilin was masked, the narrowing of his eyes was all that he needed to do to convey much of what he was thinking. "King Oogtar is young; he is still malleable," he said simply. However, even Qilin knew that it wasn't so simple as that.

"Malleable though he may be, do not mistake this for gullibility or timidity," Synturo added, and if anyone knew the truth of the statement, it was the speaker. It wasn't lost on anyone gathered at this meeting that Synturo had joined his forces with the Syndicate at the tender age of sixteen. That the Mujin Dynasty was on par with the Chimera Clan and R-Corporation in terms of power within the Syndicate spoke volumes without him even having to say much.

And perhaps this was one reason Goodvibe begrudgingly accepted the disinherited prince's words. "He is our best chance against the Neo-Spacian," Goodvibe said, his tone acidic as he spoke. His idea to solve this problem need not be spoken aloud.

"Yes. But a show of brutality would be the worst thing we do here. This is why my father's reign was never destined to be a long or prosperous one. He punished and stifled, but not once did he reward or cultivate." The young man's wisdom couldn't be denied, which really highlighted the fact that Goodvibe was trying.

"The Amphibian Tribes should be grateful that I allow them to continue drawing breath on this Earth." Goodvibe's words were as much a threat toward the constituent leaders as it was an expression of his anger with King Oogtar.

"Some might consider that an unacceptable term and condition," Qilin returned the indirect threat with one of his own, as well as a very relevant response to the matter at hand.

"And it is with that in mind that I say we give the young Amphibian King an incentive to cooperate," Synturo suggested.

Goodvibe was perhaps galled that these two and just one other could band together and defy him directly if they so chose. However, this was exactly why he appealed to that one other at this moment. "Toussaint, what do you say in all of this?" Goodvibe asked, and the CEO of R-Corporation didn't change his expression as he answered.

"First of all, that is Commander Ristar to each and every one of you," he said, though Goodvibe was clearly accepting the unspoken challenge. "Second, on this I agree with Synturo and Qilin. King Oogtar, unfortunately, should really be handled the same way as we are handling the Neo-Spacian. That is, until we can safely proceed without either." Goodvibe was hoping Commander Ristar would veto this, but he didn't sink the petulant billionaire's mood entirely.

"Does anyone dispute the plan Qilin and I shall form?" Synturo turned to the rest of the gathered constituent leaders of the Syndicate. Though Goodvibe sat above everyone else like an Emperor would loom over his Imperial Court, the fact was that Synturo, Qilin, and Commander Ristar together perhaps held as much authority over said court as the leader himself. Seeing the three of them in full agreement, nobody else so much as raised an objection.

"In that case, Qilin, Ristar, and I shall handle this ourselves."

7:00 AM Two Days Later:
The Imperial Palace, Imara's Bedroom

Imara had no idea why, but she woke up earlier than usual. In fact, she had woken up early yesterday as well. General Mansa had willingly allowed his soul to be absorbed by a Soul Reaper, all just to ensure his two children escaped. Imara wanted to believe that she was simply impressed by the nobility and farsighted thinking of the outlaw general; after all, Esau and Ranga escaped with the survivors of the Mansa Army. Imara on some level figured there'd be more trouble from the Mansa Army later, though she was hoping that Esau and Ranga would see the losses suffered as enough of a warning.

Over and beyond anything to do with the Mansa Clan, Imara found herself thinking about her father. The dreams became a recurring event; every time Imara went to sleep, she only ever saw Raj's yellow eyes glaring into her own snake-like pair. Even when she awoke, she still vaguely felt as though Raj was somehow there in the room with her, before his "presence" exited and left her only with her guilt. She heard a knock on the door.

"Imara?" It was the Crown Prince. Imara made sure that she was fully clothed this time, before opening the door.

"Your highness, I—" Imara started, before Azuro signaled for her to stop.

"Don't worry. I'm not cutting the vacation short. In fact, given what's coming up next week, I think we all deserve a break before you have to join me for the State of the Territories Conference." Imara's snake-like pupils constricted.

"That's in a week?" Imara squeaked out.

Azuro nodded. The State of the Territories Conference was held, without fail on October thirty-first of each year to take the temperature of the Empire and its constituent leaders. That much Imara knew; but here comes what she didn't know. "I'd rather us not be mentally exhausted when we meet the Crown Princes of the Kingdoms of Paradise. What I say here could potentially sway them to petition for at least a ceasefire." Imara blinked. Though she heard everything Azuro said, what stuck out to her was the fact that the Crown Princes of Paradise were going to be here.

"The Crown Princes are going to be there? As in, even Vituo Idate?" she asked, her body going both hot and cold at once at the memory of the very handsome and powerful prince. She had mistaken him for a demigod at first, but even among those he stood out. She wouldn't voice it now, but Imara wondered how she'd handle seeing him again. She breathed a sigh of relief when Azuro took this as foresight and strategic thinking.

"Don't worry. I understand the Masai Five might be intimidating. Not to mention the memory of your previous encounter with the Masai Prince." Imara wondered how Azuro could possibly know of that, but he continued before the thought could form. "But you will not be accompanying me alone. In addition to the Grand Priest presiding over the conference, I've also taken the liberty of summoning Lugato Nderu back from the front lines." Imara had heard that name before. More importantly, Raj had told the entire Gimura Force to flee immediately if he was even rumored to be in the area during raids.

"Him?" Imara asked, to which Azuro smirked.

"But of course. Vituo seems to think that he's going to try and intimidate us into submission with a show of strength and confidence. He will see that two can play this game. Lugato by our side, I'm very sure that Vituo will be much more willing to negotiate reasonably." Azuro laughed to himself at how perfect his plan was, before turning to Imara. "Until the conference, I say we enjoy our downtime." Azuro gently rubbed Imara's shoulder, guaranteeing that she now gave him her undivided attention.

"Join me."

10:00 AM:

Elven Sanctorum Courtyard

"The State of the Territories Conference? Never imagined we'd be anywhere near that in this life," a member of the Gimura Force said.

"Oh, it gets better. Apparently, the Lugato Nderu is supposed to be present, too," another, seasoned warrior said. At this, the ten warriors that rushed to rescue Imara back in Osai appeared to become rather concerned.

"The one Raj always told us to flee at the mention of?" a younger fighter said.

"Yeah, that's him," another said.

"If Imara was the one in danger, we'd have to defy that order," yet another said, and this caused the rest of the platoon to unanimously agree.

"Why exactly were we taking orders from Raj, again? Imara could have easily had us kill him any time she wanted," one of the younger members asked what every single person on the Force wondered ever since the day Imara turned fifteen and hit puberty as she did.

"I can't believe Raj actually tried to shave her beautiful hair!" another angrily remembered.

"That was the one time we shouldn't have listened to Imara. We'd have killed him then and there and set her free," yet another warrior angrily reminisced.

"Bet you Raj never even looked at Imara's hair ever again. Come to think of it, he didn't even so much as lay a hand on Imara after that day until . . ." the general anger at their former leader returned.

For two years, Raj was simply content to insult and emotionally batter his only daughter. But the day he hit her again was the day Hassan pointed his blade at his father. "The boy should have killed him then. We should have killed him then!" one particularly experienced crewmember said. "But in the end, we made good on avenging the abuse she suffered, didn't we?" The few days the Gimura Force spent in prison were spent exacting justice upon Raj for the way he treated the one young, unmarried female in their platoon. As they laughed at the recollections of what they put upon the disgraced leader, the camaraderie was interrupted.

"So, we're talking about the ugly prom date?" Torune asked, and the glares he got from some of the more hot-blooded Gimura Force crewmembers would have perhaps warned away most people.

"That 'ugly prom date' saved your life. And the worthless lives of your cronies. You'd do well to refer to her as 'Priestess Gimura' from now on," the guy who mentioned Raj's attempt to shave Imara's head spoke up, stepping forward.

"Sol, he's not worth it," one of the more level-headed crew members attempted, but Sol simply squared up with Torune. His squad might have made a move, if they didn't see the rest of the Gimura Force watching.

"No! You know what? Just like with Raj, I'm sick and tired of having to put up with garbage elven beings like you going at good women like Imara," Solom said, and it wasn't like the rest of the Gimura Force disagreed. Matter of fact, even the one who tried to diffuse the situation quickly found himself concurring.

Torune simply readied some chi in his hands, though it was noticed that his fist shook. Sol didn't care; not in the least. "Oh, so you think you're a man? Is this you defending the ugly lady's honor?!" Torune challenged, and he did his best to hide a gulp of fear when Sol got closer to him. "You want to go to hell that badly? Then go ahead. And make sure you prepare a seat for your stupid sex toy Imara," Torune said, taking a step back and summoning his tonfa. Leo and Shamir both stepped up, but even with their own weapons summoned they were not in any hurry to step between Sol and Torune.

Especially as Sol started to laugh; a crazed and bloodthirsty laugh that indicated that he was just dying to die and take someone with him. "Oh, where Imara is going, we will never be able to follow. Where she's going, it will be archangels and the seraphim preparing for her arrival. And they will have a good sixty-five or so years to prepare for the demi-goddess to return." As Sol got closer and Leo and Shamir both began to back away, Torune finally faltered.

"Stay back!" Torune said, his chi turning into Nuclear Conversion as Sol got closer.

"But not one of us here would be welcome where she will go, Torune. Hell is where we're going."

The crazed look in Sol's eyes said it all, and he seemed almost disappointed that Torune didn't pop off the way he normally would on Imara. In any case, the entire Gimura Force had been moving to surround Torune and his squad; there was nowhere for the former street toughs to run. "I hear that hell is a place for people just like us. People who have butchered their own clans alive; people who plundered entire villages out of greed or even just spite; people who have victimized and destroyed innocents just because of how they felt at the time. People who'd join and then enable a spoiled nobleman in throwing a destructive, eight-year temper tantrum over some politicking not swinging his way. Oh yes, every single member of the Gimura Force belongs there for the sins we've committed. We'll fit right in."

The rest of the Gimura Force closed in, and now the whimpers of fear from Ghinjo, the Otunga Brothers, and Sekai became audible. "But for you, Torune? You and your butt-buddies are gonna have a long and painful eternity!"

With that, Sol made his move.

10:05 AM:
Lake of Oracles

"Every time," Azuro said as Imara once again beat him in a game of Water Sniping.

"What can I say? My mom's the best shooter in the Elven Territories, and she taught me well," Imara said with a smile. Azuro chuckled to himself.

"To think a human woman holds that title," the Elven Crown Prince said humorously. Imara had never seen Azuro as loosened up as he was at this moment, and she got the distinct impression that this was reserved only for those closest to him. In fact, she wondered if the Empress ever saw this side of her son too often.

Just as Azuro and Imara were about to set up for another round, they were interrupted by a voice that Imara would normally have dreaded to hear. That is, if and only if she had still been an outlaw. "Ah, so this is where you went. Never took you for one to slack off, your highness." Imara and Azuro turned around, and saw two familiar faces, alongside Zume.

"Ah, Lugo. You made it after all," Azuro said, doing his best to avoid looking at Zume or the girl next to him. Lugato Nderu, or Lugo as Azuro referred to him, was undoubtedly Zume's older brother. He essentially looked like what would happen if Zume's eyes were normal, but the girl next to Zume clearly had the same mental handicap that her brother did. Imara couldn't believe this, but she actually felt sorry for Zume's sister. Though her own snake-like eyes could be jarring to most, at least her eyes didn't float around independently of one another when they weren't in use as Zume and his sister's tended to.

"Of course. The Empress decided I needed a break, after. Zume, Auri, bow to the Crown Prince," Lugo prompted, and his two younger siblings followed.

"He's our big brother," Imara heard, though no one spoke. That wasn't Lugo or Azuro's voice, so there was only one person who transmitted that thought to Imara. Before Imara could think of a response, Lugo actually spoke up.

"And you . . ." he asked, and being under the great Lugato Nderu's gaze was intimidating to say the least.

"I've heard much about you, even before your surrender to the Crown," Lugo said, and Imara resisted the urge to look away. "No one taught you how to use the Elemental Conversions, did they? Nor did anyone teach you how to use Physical or Spectral Conversions, I also presume?" Lugo asked, and Imara shrugged.

"I just studied some books on Sorcery. Especially when Dad didn't allow me or mom to train with the rest of the Force."

Lugo had an idea of just why exactly that was. Perhaps to others, Imara's eyes and nose were off-putting and unattractive. However, Lugo saw worse facial deformities within his own clan each and every day. In fact, Imara's snake-like eyes and pointed nose and ears were less distracting than Zume and Auri's crossed and lazy eyes that seemed to float independently of each other when they weren't focused. It is this reason that Lugo realized just why the leader of a platoon of bandits would be correct to fear his position being usurped by his daughter or wife, intentionally or otherwise.

"I see. And this was enough to allow you to wield a Troll Scimitar," Lugo said, remembering his training days and just how impressed his instructors were during his days in Sorcery School. "You'd have broken all kinds of records, for sure," Lugo said, as he turned to Azuro. "Your highness, how many of the Basic Elements have you mastered? Have you caught up to the Empress yet?" Azuro's face turned red at the question.

"Mom has been training in sorcery longer than the both of us have been alive, Lugo," Azuro indignantly informed, and from Lugo's smirk it was clear that he was just taunting the teenaged future Emperor. Zume and Auri both suppressed giggles at this.

"Have you at least caught up to Zume and Auri yet?" Lugo asked, and Azuro's blush darkened even more.

But before he could answer, a very powerful explosion sounded off in the background. Everyone immediately turned to the source, sensing that the explosion was a Nuclear Conversion technique being used. Azuro's pupils constricted when he saw that the explosion was just above the Sanctorum Temple grounds, as he realized exactly what this more than likely meant. The fierce, more intense expressions on Zume and Auri's faces also indicated that they both knew exactly what was happening. But it'd be Lugo who said what they were all thinking.

"We're gonna need to address that," he said simply, as he prepared to teleport them to the Temple.

10:08 AM:

Elven Santorum Courtyard

Imara blinked, and she was back at the Elven Sanctorum. Imara felt Lugo's chi activate and swore that it felt similar to the one emanating from the Troll Scimitar she wielded. However, his chi still very clearly belonged to an Elven being. She was tempted to ask a really stupid question, but soon she was struck dumb by what she witnessed the next moment.

What Imara thought was an energy blast was in fact Leo being shunted clear over her head, and once she made that assessment she now looked back to the action.

Torune was down, his hands still glowing from the Nuclear chi beam he fired. Imara immediately recognized Sol was the only one fighting, as the rest of the Gimura Force cheered and rooted for him to handle Torune's remaining squad. Now with Leo's rifle, Sol proceeded to use it as a club to manage numbers as he smashed both Otunga brothers in the throat. Once those two were knocked away, Sol jumped over a sneak attack from Sekai, and promptly guillotined the rifle down on his neck. Ghinjo and Shamir swung their clubs, which only prompted Solomon to jump over their attacks and level them both with a split kick. It was a wonder why Sekai even got up, because as soon as he did Sol launched him clear over Imara's head.

"That's enough!" Imara called out as she saw Sol point the rifle at Torune. She raised her voice, and every single member of the Gimura Force fell silent; all jeers, cheers, and laughter stopped. And then the focus was directed to the man standing beside Imara.

"That's . . ." one of them said, and it didn't take long for the rest of Imara's platoon to recognize Lugato Nderu.

"You have some nerve, showing your face around here!" Sol said, pointing the assault rifle at Lugo. Lugo resisted the urge to laugh; he needed to diffuse the situation, not mock the stupidity of someone trying to threaten him with a mere firearm. Zume and Auri tilted their heads inquisitively as they tried to figure out what exactly Sol's plan was in this instance.

"Sol! Stop!" Imara shouted. Sol hadn't pulled the trigger yet, but he noticeably hesitated. "He's on our side now, remember?" Imara gently explained, to which Sol looked at the still fallen Torune.

"But . . . the Mujin bastard—" Azuro interrupted.

"Is no longer your concern," Azuro said. At this, Torune felt it safe to recover. "Torune's fate is Imara's decision, and Imara's decision alone," he said, and Torune couldn't help but remember the Empress's words from that dreadful day.

"Are you kidding me?!" Torune barked out, forgetting that he was talking to the Crown Prince. Azuro narrowed his eyes.

"Do you prefer life in prison? Do you prefer to have your chi forcibly harnessed to be used in service to the Empress?" Imara blinked at hearing that; a question about the Gimura Force seals that her personal platoon used in the Empress's service had continued to burn away at her mind. However, Torune's words continued to spew out of his mouth.

"Just kill me already!" Torune said, earning Zume and Auri's disapproving stare.

"Well, Priestess Gimura? You heard him. He requests his own execution," Azuro responded. Imara began to think.

"Hmmm . . . It might solve some problems . . ." Imara pondered.

However, Torune was not about to let her finish. Before he himself even realized what he was doing, his energy turned into Nuclear Conversion yet again and he pointed his energy beam at Zume and Auri. Even Torune's squad were shocked and surprised by this action; Zume and Auri failed to act in time to the surprise attack.

Not that they needed to be worried. As quickly as Torune fired was about as quickly as the nuclear energy beam was dissipated. "What—?" Torune managed, before he found himself floating in mid-air.

"You really are a fool, to attack my younger brother and sister like that," Lugo said, and it was at this moment that Torune realized that it was him that was now holding him in mid-air. As Imara dissipated Hajitar's Shield, she could now confirm beyond a shadow of a doubt.

"Is that . . . is that Universal chi you're using?" Imara asked aloud in awe.

"Universal Force, specifically," Lugo answered with a clear edge of false modesty. "Now, which way is Hafifu Village? I need to know in which general direction to demonstrate the Universal Push to the next Grand Priestess," Lugo asked, and Torune gasped in abject horror. His wits left him as he began to panic and squirm helplessly in mid-air.

"Oh, no need to do that just yet, Lugo," Imara said in a very singsong voice. It wasn't lost on Torune that Imara emphasized the part about just yet. Zume and Auri appeared to become very enthralled at Imara's words.

Torune's heart sank when he saw his squad conspicuously slink out of view to their escape. The Gimura Force didn't follow them; they were eager to see what was going to happen to Torune. "I'm interested in hearing what you have to say. I want to know. Why do you hate me so much?" she asked solemnly, her voice as gentle as she could make it. Imara really wanted to know; it was lost on everyone present why she even cared.

Torune, most of all, was baffled by this. "You care, huh?" Torune sarcastically quipped as he tried to sound defiant, but even Zume and Auri wondered why he bothered. Lugo was tempted to close his hand and crush Torune's windpipe with the Universal Crush, but he simply looked to Imara.

"Yes, I do. From what I see, much more than most would. And perhaps that is the source of your anger toward me?" she said. Torune twitched at these words; he did his best to hide it, but his face betrayed him for just a moment. Because the next moment the bravado returned.

"No, you don't, you ugly wench! You see me the way my so-called 'cousin' does. The way the Grand Priest does," Torune seethed, and now he got going. "And especially him!" Torune couldn't move, but his eyes were directed at the one holding him with Universal Force. "You all think that you're better than me! I know you do! You do!" Torune looked at Azuro. "You do!" He then glowered at Lugo, his eyes feeling as though they were tearing up. But he refused to let any tears fall. "And especially you!" he said, his eyes meeting Imara's. Imara's face softened as he spoke.

"Your father rebelled against the Emperor! Attempted to kill the Empress! Yet, here you are taking my spot as the next Grand Priest! Here you are seducing your way to the crown!" Azuro blinked at hearing Torune's words. "And now you stand with yet another of your boy toys acting as though you care? You, who waltzes back into the Imperial Court because you're 'talented' and born from a noble clan, stands there and acts high and mighty while these men of yours hold me hostage?!" Torune's tears began to fall despite himself.

"Well, what are you waiting for?! Do it!" Torune demanded. Sol and the rest of the Gimura Force scoffed at this display. Even Lugo, Zume, and Auri were unmoved by this, but it'd be Azuro who spoke up.

"Imara?" he prompted, and the young priestess hesitated. She took a breath.

"Teleport him back to Hafifu Village, alongside the rest of his squad. We'll decide their fate after the State of the Territories Conference," Imara declared. Lugo's arm tensed for just a moment, before realizing that the next Grand Priestess technically outranked him and therefore, he had to follow her orders.

With an exasperated huff, Lugo teleported Torune out of the Sanctorum.

7:30 PM that Same Day:
The Beaches of Osai County

Ron and Koroa both looked over the Elven Territories' westernmost city; Osai was aptly named for its proximity to the ocean. Due to being the next chancellor, the rebuilding of her home city was practically a priority for the imperial workforce. Though a few buildings were destroyed, and some casualties were suffered due to the surprise attack, much of the civilian body was saved due to her father's quick thinking. However, just how close to death he and the rest of Koroa's family came to having their life forces extracted had weighed heavily on her for the past two days.

"So, the State of the Territories conference is coming up, I hear," Ron broke the tension. Koroa took a breath; despite the "vacation" she was afforded, she seemed almost disengaged.

"Yeah . . . The Crown Prince's first time presiding over it. Hopefully, the heirs to the Kingdoms of Paradise showing up means that they are interested in at least a ceasefire." Koroa tried to sound hopeful, but even the dead could see and hear just how little faith she had that the Elf-Changeling Wars would end in their generation.

So, Ron definitely wasn't fooled. "Not gonna lie, I was fully prepared to end my life in a dungeon somewhere, given that it was only a matter of time before Raj killed Imara while one of the guys weren't looking. And then, when they killed Raj for it and surrendered to the crown, that'd be the last time I saw the light of day," Ron said jovially, but with a hint of sadness to his voice. "But now, here we are. Imara will be sitting beside the Crown Prince and current Grand Priest as they preside over an international conference. If that isn't proof that major change is possible in a short time, I don't know what is."

Ron's words were genuine, but Koroa wasn't so easily convinced. "I'd have a little more faith if the Crown Prince did. There's a reason he's summoned Lugo from the front lines for this conference." Now that one made Ron do a double take.

"Wait, Lugo? As in, Lugato Nderu?" Ron said, his voice quite fragile as he spoke.

"Yep," Koroa nodded. Ron, however, was still holding out hope that he misheard her.

"The guy also known as the Executioner of Ten Thousand, the guy who once stood against the entire Masai Five and won, and the guy that often single-handedly stopped the rebellions that plagued Emperor Mujin-Anmin's reign? One of whom was even the reason Raj and my father were leading a bandit force for the last eight years? That Lugato Nderu?" Ron confirmed, though the fear in his voice said it all.

"You and the rest of the Gimura Force aren't rebels anymore, Ron. You have nothing to fear from Lugo any longer," Koroa reassured.

"I know, but Dad would always tell us to flee no matter what, if Lugo was reported to be anywhere near the area. We had to stop Raj from trying to challenge him again." Koroa's mouth fell open at the idea of Raj attempting to challenge Lugo again.

"Did . . . did he have a death wish?" she asked, to which Ron shrugged.

"More like an issue of pride. As we've seen with Torune and his flunkies, those two things might not be mutually exclusive." Ron laughed.

Before the conversation could continue, Koroa and Ron's C-Rings rang. It was Imara, and the two of them answered in short order.

"How's your vacation, Imara?" Ron asked before Imara could say anything.

"Oh, I'm just fine. Mostly just spending some time with the Crown Prince and his inner circle." Imara hadn't meant it to sound as pompous as it did, but Ron and Koroa exchanged glances.

"And your father wrote you off as a failure. Jokes on him, isn't it?" Ron said with a laugh. Imara hesitated for a moment, before regaining her composure.

"Dad was never one to take a joke too well," Imara reminisced. And Ron was happy her mood didn't plummet this time.

"And it was the main reason he was destined to lose eventually," Ron concurred.

"He and Torune have that much in common. Speaking of Torune . . ." Ron and Koroa both sighed at what they knew was coming. "He's been expelled from the Sanctorum entirely. After the State of the Territories Conference, I'm going to sentence him," Imara said. Ron was just happy to hear the good news of Torune finally being removed; that was one problem that wouldn't be a concern after October thirty-first. However, Koroa voiced her reaction to the bad news of Imara's statement.

"Imara, Torune has more than deserved imprisonment or worse by this point," Koroa informed, and Imara paused.

"I know. I really do," she said. Ron knew her well.

"But . . .?" he began for her, and the Grand-Priestess-to-be simply sighed.

"He needs help. Just as Dad did. Just as quite a few others did. Perhaps I can save him this time, now that he's lost everything and hit rock bottom. Perhaps this is the wake-up call he needed . . ." Imara said. Ron and Koroa began to roll their eyes at this.

"Seriously, Imara?" Koroa asked with great incredulity. Ron, however, didn't seem the least bit surprised.

"Okay, this has to be said. You're only going to regret this if you show this bastard any mercy. You showed Raj mercy and look how he repaid you for it." Imara's face said it all; even if the hologram wasn't visible Ron could practically hear the frown on her face form.

"I know, but—" Imara started. Ron didn't let her finish.

"But what? What reason do you have to spare him? He'd never show you this kind of mercy. He'd do his worst to you without even thinking twice and laugh about it to his friends!" Ron said, the anger in his voice apparent.

"Ron . . . I . . . I don't know, okay? I just . . . he's a hurt soul who needs to be healed, just as Dad needed it," Imara said, and Ron laughed bitterly.

"Imara, wherever you sent Torune, he's probably plotting against you as we speak!"

6:30 AM the Next Morning:
Hafifu Village Outskirts

"We need to solve this! We need to solve this now!" Leo said, the panic in his voice obvious as he paced back and forth.

"Leo, calm down, man. The only thing we can do now is handle the issue at hand," Sekai said, and if Leo was going to direct his wrath to him, he was interrupted by Shamir.

"And the issue at hand would be Torune. He's the reason we're in this predicament," Shamir said calmly.

At this, the rest of Torune's former clique concurred. "Yeah, he's the one who got us in this mess in the first place!" Jomo said.

"He just couldn't leave that ugly tramp alone!" Jotaro remembered.

"We all know he just wanted her attention," Ghinjo added. However, Shamir and Sekai became the voices of reason yet again.

"Whatever his reasons, he's now put our heads on the chopping block. There's only one thing to do in this case," Shamir said, and the feeling of blood lusted optimism immediately spread throughout the gathered ex-Sanctorum members. Torune had cost them positions within the Elven Sanctorum; he had cost them the highest honor ones such as they could hope to achieve.

"Yeah, he's always holding his 'charity' over our heads and talking about how he's the reason we were even chosen for the Sanctorum. But he can't even keep his own position secure!" Leo vented. The rest of the clique remembered that it was indeed Torune who guaranteed them positions of high prestige and power within the Sanctorum; all of them had in fact never attended Sorcery School. That said, this was in the past. And in the present, their very lives were hanging in the balance because of him.

"Don't worry though. That's why we are here this morning. We're gonna pay him a visit and show him just how we 'take care' of those who cost us like he did," Shamir said, and he found no complaints from anyone present.

"An interesting plan," a calm, sardonic, powerful, yet unseen voice sounded. Torune's former squad all turned around, assuming their fighting stances. It was the last mistake they would ever make.

October 30th

Imara woke up in the middle of a Gimurdina Prison Camp. Her eyes immediately constricted from fear as she realized that she was surrounded by the worst convicts in the Elven Territories. Thankfully, she was fully clothed; never had she been more thankful for her off-putting face than she was at this moment. The men around her did not so much as look her way, however. Mostly because they were more interested in whoever they were swarming and attacking. Imara found herself moving toward the commotion involuntarily, despite every single urge in her body telling her to stay where she was. In fact, her body seemed to actively defy every thought she had; it felt as though she were under an Illusion more than she was dreaming.

In either case, Imara's pupils constricted when she saw just why these prisoners were more interested in their quarry than in the one female in the prison. In fact, the very fact that she was female was the reason this one prisoner was being attacked.

"LOOK WHAT YOU'VE DONE TO ME, YOU UGLY FAILURE!" Raj's voice sounded, drowning out the insults and jeers from the other prisoners. "YOU CONTINUE TO LEAVE ME HERE, AND THIS IS WHAT THEY'RE DOING TO ME!"

Imara winced at the brutality that her restrained father endured. The other prisoners jeered and spat at the man as they took their fun in beating him. "So, you like to abuse little girls, huh?" one called as they kicked Raj in the teeth, knocking them all out.

"You're supposed to be her father!" another accused as he broke Raj's ribs.

"You think you're gonna hurt your wife and daughter and get away with it!?" another said as he gouged out Raj's eyes. Imara was happy she could turn her head at the sight. But she couldn't drown out Raj's voice.

"Are you satisfied now!? You killed me! Left me here to this fate! You now have what you wanted, you evil failure! Hope you enjoy the rest of your pathetic, ungrateful life!"

7:30 AM:

Imara's Bedroom

Imara was jolted awake. She looked around and sighed in relief when she realized that it was just a dream. However, as soon as she came to that realization, she felt something . . . odd. The seal that the Imperial Court issued to her was no longer emanating that strange, yet familiar Spectral aura. If she didn't know better, she might have sworn that the chi emanating from the seals of the reformed Gimura Force had belonged to someone she might have known.

But now, however, the Spectral chi that she felt from her seal felt almost artificial; there was no longer an alive aspect to it. She went to the bathroom and looked herself over in the mirror. Remembering her dream from just a moment ago, Imara truly evaluated her looks objectively for the first time in the two months since she and the Gimura Force surrendered to the Imperial Court.

And objectively speaking, Imara could not deny that she inherited the best of both sides of her clan. Between her mother Penelope and her Aunt Izuna, Imara was blessed with a perfect physical amalgamation of two of the most beautiful women the

Elven Territories had produced in recent memory. Her olive skin was complemented greatly by her luscious jet-black hair; her lips were full, naturally pink and enticing; her chest was perky, supple and was in fact bigger than her aunt's; her rounded and well-set hips led down to her well-toned and powerfully muscled legs. Even if she wasn't so ashamed of her eyes and nose, Imara could see that the good definitely outweighed the bad.

Her snake-like eyes and pointed nose and ears were the only things that could truly be said to be jarring. However, even with these two "flaws," Imara counted herself lucky. Given that she was half-human and half-elf, she honestly wondered how she didn't end up like Zume, Auri, or the vast majority of elven-human hybrids. She suspected that it might have been for the same reason that she alone among her clan was as talented with as many Conversions of chi as she was.

Imara's mind felt itself becoming more and more at peace as she showered. Her body felt as though a great weight was lifted from upon her as she did her morning stretches and then got dressed. And as she left her room, she felt as though it were truly a new day and the beginning of a new era.

That is, until she stepped outside her door. Standing in front of her was the vengeful, angry face of the man she had sent home just a week ago. The man whose outbursts had cost him his position as the next Grand Priest, and then his position in the Elven Sanctorum entirely. However, his eyes and his demeanor spoke volumes about who he blamed for being sent home a week ago.

"Torune?" Imara dumbly said aloud, and he continued to glower angrily at her. "How . . . did . . ." she started, but then her throat constricted. The man with Torune was unmistakable. At first, Imara thought Azuro had welcomed his cousin, if no one else, back to the Imperial Palace. However, this man was much taller than the teenaged Crown Prince, and he was definitely possessed of more traits of his father than Azuro was. Imara froze, seeing Synturo Anmin at her door.

"Imara Gimura." Even Synturo's voice sounded like a stronger, more powerful version of his younger brother. Imara couldn't even blink as she stared up in abject fear. "Seeing you in person, I have to say that Maharajan was wrong. Very, very wrong. Your beauty will only increase with age. As will your power." Imara's pupils dilated at hearing Synturo say this; never had a compliment sounded like the worst possible omen imaginable. "You will be coming with us, Imara," Synturo said, his voice low but still forceful enough to compel Imara to move. She wished she could wake up, but the more rational part of her knew that she was no longer dreaming.

"You're right about one thing Syn," Torune said, a very ominous and cruel look in his eye. Imara realized that Torune was not looking her in the face. Even though she was dressed modestly and did not show cleavage, her curves were undeniable and impossible to hide. "Raj was very wrong. We've got some time; how about I give Imara a preview of her place in the Mujin Dynasty," Torune said, his hands inching their way toward Imara's hips.

"Torune," Synturo said, stopping his cousin in his tracks.

"Imara will be coming with us. Unmolested," Synturo said firmly. Imara never thought she'd see Torune fall in line as he did, but he only argued minimally.

"Now why do you get to keep her for yourself?" Torune whined, to which Synturo narrowed his eyes.

"Unmolested, Torune," he repeated, a more threatening edge to his voice as he stepped closer to his first cousin. If Torune was five-ten or five-eleven in his bare feet, one could see that Synturo was no shorter than six-three even on a bad day. Torune relented after a few moments before turning back to Imara.

"How . . . how did you two . . ." Imara couldn't form any more words.

"Go ahead and scream all you want. No one will be able to hear you," Synturo coldly informed.

"It'd be a pain if she tries to rile up some of that precious chi of hers," Torune said.

"The Illusion that Qilin cast can't be broken as easily as normal Illusions. Even King Oogtar and King Jabal will find this Illusion difficult to break," Synturo explained.

"I-Illusion?" Imara repeated. Synturo simply looked at her. Imara felt her insides freeze under his gaze.

"However, we can never be too sure. Place the Restrictor Seal. And only place the Restrictor Seal," Synturo ordered. Torune seemed to figure this was as good as he was going to get. The lecherous smile that spread across his face as his hands reached for Imara's sizable chest was perhaps more intimidating than the idea of having her chi forcibly suppressed.

"Synturo. Mujin," Azuro's unseen voice sounded. Torune stopped cold when he heard the Crown Prince's voice. Imara was too frozen to even appreciate the fortuitous turn of events.

"It's been a long time, baby brother," Synturo said without turning to face the new arrival. Imara's mind needed a moment to process, but she was now witnessing the reunion of Kato Mujin's two sons.

"Synturo. Mujin," Azuro repeated, his anger building up even more.

"I see Chagua hasn't returned from her Master Challenge yet." The mention of their sister did nothing to soften Azuro's anger.

"I don't need her to put you two down where you stand!" Azuro said, summoning up his chi. And upon feeling his chi activate, now Imara's mind caught up. Specifically, she felt Azuro's chi convert into an element that she had never felt from the Crown Prince in the past two months of training with him.

"Temporal Evolution?" Synturo said in surprise. He had just barely registered this development when Azuro dashed forward.

Azuro activated the Temporal Boost, and as soon as he did he dashed at his older brother. "NOW YOU DIE!" Azuro's voice echoed with the sheer power he was generating.

Imara gasped and squeezed her eyes shut at the sound of his voice. Meanwhile Torune's eyes widened in shock when he sensed that Azuro was in fact using Temporal Evolution and not any other form of Wind Conversion. In fact, Azuro's Temporal chi felt stronger and more refined than his own Nuclear Evolution; Torune's heart began to thunder in his ears as the angered Crown Prince rocketed toward him. However, his heart only had a chance to beat three times before Azuro had closed the distance and he was upon them with his strongest and most vicious punch.

But, where Torune and Imara froze, the disinherited Crown Prince had acted. As quickly as Azuro had moved, Synturo's arm had moved three times as fast and had more than enough time to divert his energized punch. And when he did, everything to the right of Azuro had been blasted into oblivion. Imara opened her eyes and was greeted with the sight of the Crown Prince looking up at his older brother with subdued horror. Azuro appeared outwardly defiant, but his eyes and trembling demeanor said so much more.

"In . . . incredible . . ." Torune said, unable to hide his awe at not only Azuro's power, but also Synturo's ability to counter and divert said power.

"No . . . no!" Imara finally said, realizing just what this meant. Synturo turned to face her; any fear she might have had for herself was instantly replaced with concern for a friend.

The buildup of chi as she summoned her Troll Scimitar was undeniable. "So, the Grand Priestess finally reveals herself," Synturo said as he admired the perfect balance of Physical, Natural, and Spectral chi.

Azuro, however, was not to be denied as he attempted to press the attack. He attempted to retract his hand. "Stop," Synturo said. He didn't bother raising his voice, so the very audible BREAK! that sounded from Azuro's arm being driven practically drowned out his speech. Azuro screamed in agony.

"AZURO!" Imara called out at seeing him fall over in agony, clutching his arm. "That's it!" she said as she ran to help her fallen friend. Torune, however, was quicker on the draw.

"Oh no you don't!" he said, as he intercepted Imara. Before he could place the Restrictor Seal on her, however, she ducked under his attack and drove the pommel of the scimitar directly into Torune's groin. She was on the mark, and the hilt made crushing contact. Torune couldn't scream, nor block the heel kick to the chin that came next. With Torune out of the way, Imara continued to charge at the disinherited prince.

Until the unexpected happened.

"Imara! No!" It was Azuro who had spoken up. Imara froze when she heard him, and then gaped in horror as he stood up shakily. His right arm quivered; his forearm was broken in at least two different places. "Synturo will die by my hand!" Azuro's emotions had gotten the best of him, and it was obvious right now.

"But . . . your highness!" Imara called out in concern. Synturo turned to his younger brother.

"Go away. You, Mother, and Chagua will have your time," Synturo warned. Azuro was only further incensed.

"MY TIME IS NOW!" Azuro said, as he lunged at Synturo with his unbroken left arm. Before his fist ever reached him, the more experienced fighter uppercut the angry Crown Prince in the chin, sending him careening down the hallway. Azuro slumped to the ground, and Imara raised her weapon.

"No! Imara, I order you to leave Synturo to me!" Azuro barked out. Imara's arms shook, as her eye twitched in hesitation. "The Clan traitor is mine!" Azuro said, once again standing up and activating the Temporal Boost. The unassisted eye was unable to see Azuro charge at his older brother, and the unassisted eye was also unable to see Synturo divert the punch he threw. However, there was no denying the powerful kick to the chest that he responded with, sending Azuro right back across the hall and against the wall on the other side yet again.

Imara's eyes teared up at seeing the hopelessness of Azuro's situation. Her legs shook; every urge in her body told her to defy the prince's orders. "He . . . he will die by my hand!" Azuro unconsciously managed. His right forearm was broken at a horrifying angle, and Azuro was barely able to pick himself back up.

"In that case . . ." Synturo calmly said as he began to walk over to his fallen brother. Imara summoned up as much chi as she could and attempted to convert her power into as much Illusion chi as possible.

"Don't waste your time, butterface," Torune said, still clearly in pain from Imara's onslaught. "You can't break the Illusion, even if you try. No one's coming to help you two, so just watch!" Imara seethed when she heard this, but she quickly found out how right Torune was. In any case, Synturo was now standing over Azuro, who seemed to look up at just the moment Imara refocused on the situation at hand.

And just as soon as he did, Azuro lunged to his feet and attempted another attack. The knee to his belly put a stop to that. Azuro coughed up blood as he began to fall forward, right into the other knee of his older brother. Before he could fall backward, Synturo pulled him back into a solid punch that took Azuro clear off his feet. He spun through the air for a full three seconds before he hit the ground.

"Why . . ." Azuro droned out, barely conscious. As if to answer, Synturo picked him up by his throat with his left hand, as he summoned some chi in his right.

"Pathetic. Just like Mother and Chagua . . ." Synturo said, his tone turning venomous. "You will never be able to beat me!" Synturo said, converting his power into Nuclear Evolution, and then forming an Energy Blade around his hand. However, before he could do anything else, Imara's footsteps got his attention.

"Maybe he could, with a little help!" Imara said, the last word of her declaration being emphasized as she swung her blade at Synturo's arm. The disinherited prince let go of his brother at just the right time to avoid having his arm chopped off. Getting some distance, Synturo turned his Energy Blade into an Energy Beam instead and fired it at his adversaries. Almost as soon as the blast left his hand did Imara summon Hajitar's Shield. The pink barrier did its job and dispelled the nuclear blast.

"Interesting," Synturo said, as Imara burst through the smoke and attempted to decapitate him with a Dragon Kick. Synturo had to teleport out of the way, and Imara rolled through to avoid crash-landing on the floor. "To force Hajitar to do your bidding, on top of wielding his weapon masterfully," Synturo said, as he dodged the fiercest of Imara's slashes. The moment Imara overcommitted, however, was the moment he teleported out of her sight.

Imara felt a sharp jab on the base of her neck before her vision began to swim. "With just a little more refinement, you will be very useful to my plans." Imara's arms suddenly became very heavy. "It's over. Don't fight," Synturo said, as Imara's legs fought a losing battle to remain capable of support. She felt as though the force of gravity acting on her had multiplied tenfold; she dropped her weapon as she staggered.

But then, just as quickly as her mind was being shut down, did she suddenly feel a surge of revitalization. The clouds that had fogged up her mind were suddenly cleared, and as her vision returned to normal, she could notice the panicked look upon Torune's face.

"Should have figured you'd strike just before the State of the Territories Conference." Imara didn't need to turn around to recognize it was Lugo's voice that sounded behind her. The look of optimism on Imara's face was priceless as Synturo took a few steps back. "Trying to kidnap the Grand Priestess and use her power to gain an edge over the Empress. Not a bad plan, Syn. Which is exactly why it was so predictable."

Torune finds his voice. "How? How did you get past the Illusion!?" Lugo began to summon up his chi; Imara felt the mixture of Physical, Natural, and Spiritual chi before she felt the result.

"All these years, and you two still know nothing of me." Lugo sounded almost disappointed that Torune even asked that question. "Imara, start healing our prince. Leave these two to me," Lugo said. Torune's arms shook, despite tightening his grip on his tonfa.

"I . . . I've always wanted to fight you!" Torune said, though it was clear that he was very, very afraid. Even Synturo just cast a side glance at the display of false bravado.

"Torune, we are not here to fight a full-scale battle. If Lugo is here, this means the Illusion is dispelled. Assuming we survive engaging him right this instant, we will not have enough power to escape the returning troops," Synturo explained as he surrounded himself and Torune in a barrier.

"Make no mistake, however. We will have our chance," the disinherited prince calmly warned, as he teleported himself and Torune out of the Imperial Palace.

And like that, disaster was averted. Imara didn't know how tense she was until she relaxed her grip on the Troll Scimitar. Her hands throbbed in pain as the instant relief washed over her. "I'm . . . I'm alive . . . I'm still here . . ." she said, more to calm herself. Lugo took a breath.

Synturo and Torune were both after Imara, he thought.

"Azuro!" Imara said, as she ran to the unconscious Crown Prince. She checked his heart and sighed in relief when she heard a heartbeat. "Okay . . ." Imara said, as she took a calming breath and begin to activate the Healer's Hand. Lugo, however, kept observing her as she worked.

I doubt she was even concerned with compatibility. Her Elemental Proclivity is probably not even the same as his, yet she's healing him with no problem. Can she use the Living Triage technique as well? Even if she can't . . . Lugo thought, as Azuro started to stir.

"You're gonna be okay. Just relax," Imara said, hoping to soothe the stirring prince. At the sound of her voice, the prince did just that.

11:00 AM:
The Meditation Garden

"I don't understand. Why would they be after me?" Imara asked once Lugo had finished explaining the situation to Ron, Koroa, Zume, and Auri. The prince would still need his rest, but Imara had healed him entirely. Everyone, especially Lugo, found it almost comical that Imara was still unable to truly appraise just how great her talent in the mystical arts truly was.

"Tell me, what do you know of the Living Triage technique?" Lugo asked. Imara wondered what this had to do with her question.

"The Living Triage?" she dumbly repeated before she seemed to remember something. "You mean this?" she said as she summoned up the characteristic blue and green aura of the Healer's Hand. However, this time she surrounded her entire body with it. Her snake-like eyes became blank, and glowed white as though she was using the Sight of Oracles. Lugo, Auri and Koroa all blinked; they could barely hide their surprise at just how pretty Imara actually was if she didn't have such off-putting eyes. Zume's mouth fell open as his own unusual and unfocused eyes snapped to full attention.

"It's not perfect, but I think I have the basics of it down." Imara was wrong; she was way past the basics.

"How long can you keep that up?" Lugo asked, to which Imara shrugged.

"I don't know. I've never needed to do so for more than five minutes at a time," she answered. Now Koroa and Auri's mouths fell open upon hearing that, joining Zume in gaping shock. Lugo's eyes visibly widened.

"Five entire minutes? Consecutively?" he asked, to which Imara nodded.

"I see," Lugo said, absorbing this information as best as he could. "Imara, have you ever considered taking the Master Challenge?" he asked. At this, Koroa found her voice.

"What can Master Sheng possibly teach Imara that she can't figure out herself?" she asked incredulously. Imara blinked.

"Master Sheng?" she asked, before an unexpected voice answered.

"Ah, so you do know how to use the Living Triage." Imara gasped, losing her concentration and dispelling the Living Triage aura involuntarily. Even Koroa and Ron had to double take at who just walked in, because they didn't expect to see any of the princes of the Kingdoms of Paradise until tomorrow. However, Zume and Auri simply stared at the new arrival with a serious ferocity. Zume especially seemed ready to attack at will when he saw the way Imara looked at the Masai Prince. Lugo, however, didn't so much as tense up.

"Yes. And from what I see she's even better at it than I am," Lugo said. However, his voice then hardened a bit. "What I don't see is Prince Azuro allowing you to be in his Meditation Gardens." He didn't make a threat; Lugo did not need to.

"We are not here to fight, Lugo. In fact, we are no longer even here to make demands. Azuro must by now be aware of just who was behind the Illusion that ensured Synturo's easy passage into the city," Vituo said, not letting his tone betray the apprehension he felt at Lugo's cavalier tone. Imara was tempted to tell Lugo to show a little more respect, until she remembered whose side she was on.

"When he wakes up, he will be informed. The question is how you know who cast the Illusion," Lugo said.

"At first, I suspected that it was the real Raj's doing, making another attempt on royalty," Vituo said, looking at Imara as he talked about her father. She couldn't muster up any anger at the handsome prince; Imara felt ashamed of her inability to override her inner feelings at a time like this. "But then, I found that Raj's power was emanating from none other than Qilin." Imara, however, wasn't so caught up in her feelings as to miss what Vituo just said.

"Qilin?" she asked, remembering that name from one of Raj's lists of bounties. "Using my dad's power?" she continued, more questions forming in her mind. Vituo simply narrowed his eyes at the sole daughter of this generation of the Gimura Clan.

"Yes . . . I knew your father was a traitor and a sorry excuse for a family man, but I hadn't quite taken him for a total coward. Perhaps you'd care to tell the truth about who was actually leading the Gimura Force that day?" Ron and Imara both blinked at this. Vituo's handsome features were unreadable, as Zume and Auri looked at one another.

"Umm, what?" Ron asked, disbelieving what he just heard. However, Vituo wasn't so easily swayed.

"The Grand Priestess knows the truth. She summoned a Thrall to impersonate her father, hence why his power level was so pitiful. And why you didn't fight your best," Vituo said, knowingly. Imara didn't quite know how to tell him this, so Ron cut in here.

"Prince, you might be giving Raj just a little too much credit, there. You know he failed Sorcery School twice, don't you?" Ron said as respectfully as he could.

"Perhaps, but she is a different story entirely," Vituo responded, as he looked over to Imara. "This woman not only wields a Troll Scimitar, but controls Hajitar's power as easily as if it were her own," he said. Zume and Auri looked at one another, as Lugo raised his eyebrow at Vituo's assessment of Imara.

"The real Raj would have been too prideful to not try his utmost against me, if for no other reason than to have the head of an Idate Clan member as a trophy." Imara's cheeks flushed red as Vituo stared into her soul. "What's more, the Illusion that Qilin was using definitely originated from the real Raj, wherever he is," Vituo said with finality. At this, Lugo finally spoke up.

"Vituo, Ron and the entire Gimura Force mutinied and turned Raj over to General Tensai. He is currently locked away in a prison camp, being experimented on by our premier scientists," Lugo explained. A very horrible realization crossed Imara's mind, one that she couldn't help but voice.

"Dad's been alive this entire time?!"

Imara's voice sounded hurt. Zume and Auri both moved to comfort her, but the stern glare on her eyes as she looked to Ron and then to Lugo for answers indicated that it was quickly being replaced with incredulity at being lied to as it concerned her father's fate. Koroa ran her hand through her bright blonde hair; a sign in her that she was uncomfortable.

Vituo seemed just as surprised as Imara was, but for a different reason. Lugo took a breath, before deciding to just be truthful. "Yes. He was, up until this morning. His vast amount of Spectral chi was being siphoned into those new seals the Empress commissioned for the reformed Gimura Force." Ron conspicuously avoided eye contact with Imara, but she'd address that one later.

"So, those dreams that I had. They were so real . . . because they were! Dad was telepathically screaming for help to the only that he knew would help him," Imara said, tears coming to her eyes. Now Zume and Auri hugged Imara in consolation as the tears fell. Lugo felt his heart twinge with guilt, especially as Imara looked to Lugo with pleading eyes.

"How long did you know?" Imara then looked to Ron and Koroa. "And did you two know?" She couldn't keep her anger. She just couldn't; not with this new knowledge.

"Even if the Grand Priest or Azuro had informed them, they were in no position to free Raj," Lugo said, hoping that it would ease Imara's grief. It had the opposite effect.

"But I could have!" she said. Even Vituo's face started to soften at what he was witnessing, and Zume and Auri simply glowered at Lugo in support of Imara.

"I'm the next Grand Priestess! I could have ordered my father free this whole time! But you, Azuro and Malkia all lied to me!" The hurt tone in her voice melted even Vituo's resolve, and he turned his back. So many memories came flooding into his mind, but this wasn't his moment. And he was not about to infringe upon Imara's.

"They lied to protect you, Imara," Lugo attempted. Zume and Auri looked at him as if to say, "Not helping!" but Imara voiced that instead.

"Protect me?! By hiding the fact that my father was being tortured and experimented on?! By giving me a seal made from said results of torture and continuing to use his platoon for your own purposes!? Or was Dad right in saying that the Anmins are as selfish as the Mujins!?" The fire in Imara's eyes burned bright, for her tears were the fuel that her anger drew from. Ron and Koroa actually felt fear at seeing Imara like this. And the power that spiked from her made even Vituo take a step back.

The Nderu siblings, however, were conspicuously unfazed. Zume and Auri looked at her with saddened expressions, but Lugo didn't let his feelings get the best of him. "Imara, how many people has your father killed, in just the eight years he was leading the Gimura Force? How many people have you yourself killed, in defense of your father?" The question pierced Imara's conviction, which simply meant the anger intensified. However, anger in itself was pretty useless.

"So what? I defend my family and my friends! As anyone would!" she argued, but then Lugo finally clenched the argument.

"Do you know how many people your father and Atto killed the day he rebelled? Do you know how many bodies the Royal Guard and I had to clean up that day? Do you know how many people's lives were ruined that day, over what amounts to your father throwing a temper tantrum over not getting his way?" Zume and Auri were now telepathically screaming in Lugo's head for him to stop, but it was clear that he wasn't.

"Not only that, when Raj broke out of prison and began his life as a bandit, who was the one who rescued you from the Empress's bondsmen?" Imara froze. She didn't want to answer, yet she could not lie. Not when one third of the answer to Lugo's question was sitting right there in the room.

"But . . ." Imara attempted, but her words died on her lips when she realized the horrible truth. Now Ron spoke up.

"Raj literally expended so much effort and took so many unnecessary risks in rescuing your brothers from the Gimurdina prison camps by himself. Meanwhile, he couldn't even take a simple detour and help Dad, Penelope, and I fight off ten measly bounty hunters before doing so? Come on, Imara. Use your head."

And Imara did. She thought about all the times Raj had left her to her fate, and just how often he didn't care if she lived or died. She thought about how much he hated her, and how her success often just angered him further. After his rebellion eight years ago, Raj no longer had any love for his daughter.

But that was just it; Imara then remembered what he was like before his failed attempt on the crown. Imara knew Raj loved her deep down because he once showed it. She could not forget those times; she did not want to remember anything about him but those times.

"Just . . . just leave me alone!" Imara said, as she teleported out of the Meditation Gardens.

Zume angrily weaved some hand signs to Lugo as soon as he was looking at him, but it was not his older brother who answered. "No, no, Zume. It needed to be said. Imara's grief will pass, but what Raj did to her will take some time to truly heal. It always hurts worst before the mending process begins."

Zume and Auri both did a double take, as Lugo blinked. Auri's surprised face didn't change, as she weaved more hand signs. And Ron didn't miss a beat. "Yes, I can understand Elven Sign language. Can't speak it well, but I can understand you perfectly," he responded aloud.

"Well, that's . . . unexpected," Koroa said, clearly impressed that Ron managed to learn.

Zume and Auri both weaved the exact same hand signs, in perfect unison. "Because neither of you asked or even showed that you could before now. I think we'd have communicated much easier if Zume had just tried," Ron responded, before turning back to Lugo.

"In any case, we should just give Imara some time. Hopefully, this doesn't affect the State of the Territories Conference tomorrow."

8:00 AM the Next Morning:
The Conference Pavilion

The Weather Corps had definitely done their job in ensuring that it would be a beautiful day for the conference. Imara never thought she'd see this many royal figures and leadership magnates in one setting, let alone be the one presiding over them. But here she was, standing with the current Grand Priest, as his top apprentice and his chosen successor. Moreover, she stood just above Lugo, Zume, and Auri as she first looked to her left, where the heirs to the five Kingdoms of Paradise stood in their own regal majesty. To the furthest left was the statuesque Princess Sultana Msalti of the Kanuri Kingdom, and if there was ever anyone fit to be named "Queen" in the language, there she was. Her hair was tied back, but the large bun it formed indicated that it was no shorter than Imara's nearly waist length hair.

Next to Sultana was the solidly built, steadfast Prince Kalin Odessa of the Hesura Kingdom. One would be forgiven for confusing him for an Asian Emperor as opposed to a Changeling prince, given his Asiatic features and skin tone as well as his reddish-brown hair.

Either way, this was a man that commanded the utmost of fealty and respect whenever he was in a given room.

Not that the much taller, stronger man next to him was any less regal-bearing and intimidating. His skin was a little lighter than Vituo's, but his dreads were as voluminous as the Masai prince's. Unlike Vituo, however, Tometai "Tome" Jubei of the Yorura Kingdom was a far more imposing presence than the comely and inviting prince. Standing at six-four and being no lighter than 260 pounds, Prince Tome was the largest of the gathered Changeling princes.

Almost as though to contrast him entirely, Princess Kaguya Kinsuo of the Hutu was the shortest and youngest of the royal representatives at five-five. However, this was not by any means a sign of weakness; in fact, this young, sturdy woman looked as though she'd be quicker to action than the other three heirs to the kingdoms. Imara began to wonder if she wasn't the true power in the Hutu Kingdom, even with Emperor Kinsuo being alive and well.

But pointedly, it was Prince Vituo Idate of the Masai Kingdom who would be speaking for his and the other four Kingdoms of Paradise. And pointedly, the one who spoke for the Elven Territories' ancestral adversaries would only speak when the Grand Priest dictated that it was his turn. "Imara. Now that the foreign representatives are here . . ." the Grand Priest prompted. Imara looked to Lugo, who confirmed that she would be the one to do the honors.

"Of course," she said, as she cleared her throat. "Welcome to the State of the Territories Conference. As you five are aware, this is normally a meeting of the most powerful leaders within the territories, some of whom are monarchs in their own right and therefore considered to be Her Majesty's equal."

Imara truly believed what she just said, but the five Changelings in front of her fought to keep the snarky responses from etching onto their faces. Even the Grand Priest himself wondered just how "equal" the non-Elf monarchs truly were to Malkia.

"However, the Empress is honored to know that peaceful negotiations to end ancestral conflicts are taking place. May this conference see every side achieve a favorable outcome," Imara said, and upon finishing her recital the cue was given for the subordinate monarchs of the Elven Crown to make their appearance, and then for the Chancellor and Grand Marshal to make their appearances.

As they entered the Conference Pavillion, Imara couldn't help but notice the tension filling the air. Azuro, Chancellor Harakaze, and Grand Marshal Tensai seemed almost anxious about what was to come; Empress Malkia was conspicuously absent from this year's conference. They all knew where she was and what she was doing; it wasn't lost on the Changeling heirs that the Empress had ensured that Lugo, Zume, and Auri were in attendance while she herself remained on the battlefield.

"Hi, Zume! Hi Auri!" the Amphibian King called out, his words breaking right through the tension before the Subterranean King Abdul Kidoko could deliver a formal greeting. Imara blinked at just how informal the hulking subordinate monarch was in this situation. In fact, the giant hominid currently tickling, play-wrestling, and laughing childishly with Zume and Auri was a surprise in general. The giant monster of a man was no less than seven feet tall and not an ounce lighter than five hundred pounds. His body was almost spherical; one would not be surprised if he could retract his arms and legs and simply roll faster than he could run.

Then his own snake-like eyes met Imara's. Most Amphibians were possessed of either snake-like or chameleon-like ocular organs, but this giant's eyes stood out even to that because of the fact that they glowed rainbow. "Hey, Zume, who's the lady? I don't think I've seen her before." Even this giant's voice was exactly the kind you'd expect to come out of a fat, brutish dullard that would have difficulty doing such actions as thinking or being considerate. Imara felt her skin crawl at how he looked at her; this giant was staring at her as if she was the most delectable and exotic delicacy he had ever laid eyes on.

The Grand Priest stepped forward. "King Oogtar, the woman you are speaking to is my successor, and therefore is presiding over the State of the Territories Conference. Show Priestess Gimura the proper respect," he warned, to which the giant of that name shrugged.

"Ah, come on Gari. Learn to lighten up a bit. Empress Malkia wouldn't be so uptight, so neither should you." Imara blinked.

"King Oogtar?" she found herself asking aloud, despite trying to keep a professional tone where the jolly ton of fun didn't. Oogtar's attention turned back to her, and his gaze made her feel as though she were nude and embarrassed.

"That's right. The King of the Amphibian Tribes, right here. And I should have figured a classy lady like you would be super important. Empress Malkia knows how to choose her Court Leaders." Azuro knew that was directed at him, and it didn't help that Zume and Auri giggled at the veiled insult. The Changeling heirs were dumbstruck at the behavior of this lumbering Amphibian; they wondered how he could be a king.

"Also, I think I have heard of you. You're the Master Sorceress who can wield a Troll Scimitar, aren't you?" he asked.

"I . . . I wouldn't call myself a master, per say . . ." Imara answered. Vituo wondered just how much of Imara's modesty was genuine. In fact, he wondered if she knew just what she was saying each time she confirmed that she could in fact wield an Accursed Armament.

"Well?" Oogtar prompted. Imara looked to Azuro, then to the Nderu siblings. They all nodded.

And when they did, Imara summoned her signature weapon. The reactions to this were mixed. Azuro preened just a bit at just how fearful the Changelings became at seeing Imara hold the Troll Scimitar with no problems whatsoever. Sultana's mouth dropped open for just a moment, before she recomposed herself. Kaguya, Kalin, and Tome gasped in surprise, but Vituo's response was the most muted yet most noticeable, due mostly to Imara looking right at him as she held up her weapon.

"Oh wow. That looks cool," Oogtar said, as he laughed the most stereotypically dim-witted laugh one could ever hear. "Looks like Lugo and I aren't the only ones to have completed the Master Challenge." Now it was Vituo's turn to look stunned, but unlike Sultana he couldn't recompose himself in time.

"Excuse me?" he said. Oogtar, however, ignored him.

"Can I hold it?" he asked, holding out his hand.

Imara blinked. "Excuse you?" she responded. Oogtar didn't so much as change his expression.

"I just want to hold it and take a better look. You don't mind, do you?" he said, clearly not comprehending what he was asking for.

"Oogtar, you can't possibly—" the Grand Priest started, but Lugo stopped him.

"Actually, I want to see how Oogtar plans to hold it," Lugo said, with a look that just screamed, "two can play this game." Imara's pupils dilated at what Lugo just said. Azuro, the Grand Priest, the Chancellor, and the Grand Marshal all turned to look at Lugo.

However, Zume and Auri were pointedly just as calm as Lugo was when he spoke. "Don't worry. If anything . . . untoward happens, we're right here," he reassured. Imara hesitated, just long enough for the Changelings to wonder what Lugo meant by "we." But not long enough to actually voice that question, because in the next moment, Imara handed Oogtar the feared Troll Scimitar.

And, fearing nothing whatsoever, the big man grabbed hold of it.

A severe chill was sent through the entire meeting. All except the Nderu siblings felt their blood go cold at this moment, for what happened next, they could never prepare for if they had two lifetimes. However, they only had a split second to brace themselves for what happened next.

And what happened was . . . nothing at all. Hajitar's power did not overtake the hulking brute of a king; Oogtar's eyes didn't even so much as twitch. Imara's mouth fell open at the sight of this, despite suspecting something was different about his chi. The Grand Priest, the Grand Marshal, the Chancellor, and especially Azuro were struck dumb at seeing that Oogtar was not being corrupted.

If anything, as Oogtar examined it, the Troll Scimitar quickly reformed and resized itself to accommodate him as opposed to the other way around.

"Oh yeah, this is the real deal. Given the temper, the reinforced hilt and especially the pink jewel embedding in the hilt, I'm gonna say . . . that Hajitar is sealed in here," Oogtar guessed.

"How . . . how can you possibly know that?" Imara asked in a tiny voice. She didn't see Lugo, Zume, and Auri hide smiles at the situation. Oogtar shrugged.

"Isn't hard to figure out. Gengetsu is blue, Mtanga is purple, Sengaru is yellow, and Kagerou is green. Hajitar is pink, so . . ." Oogtar's logic wasn't incorrect, but now Vituo asked the pertinent question.

"How? How can you wield this weapon so easily?" he asked incredulously. Oogtar blinked.

"Umm . . . Clearly, I have the ability to use Universal chi and know the Impulse Suppression Seal well enough to keep Hajitar from acting up. Just like Hajitar just now, you people ask some of the most obvious questions."

Oogtar continued to examine the Troll Scimitar, and finally held it with both hands. "I've got to say, there's some serious power contained in this weapon. Even compared to the other four Troll

Scimitars, Hajitar's power is particularly fierce and imposing. I could barely hear myself think when I first got my hands on this weapon. I had to ask Zume and Auri to repeat themselves once I disconnected Hajitar's line." The Changelings and the Elven Imperial Court stared disbelievingly at hearing Oogtar imply Zume and Auri were capable of speech of any kind. Oogtar looked at Imara.

"No wonder Syn and Qilin were so willing to take such a risk to bring you to his side. Exceptional leadership skills, the beauty of a goddess, as well as power that not even the Neo-Spacians or the Galaticans could stand against . . . And this is before you've even set foot in Master Sheng's dimension."

Vituo felt his blood go cold at the assessment of Imara. He was not convinced that Raj would be so dumb as to mistreat and abuse the one who could have helped him take over the Elven Territories. No, the one who could have helped him seize the world if he so chose. "Im . . . Imara, tell me the truth. Why. Did. You. Hold back?" Vituo asked forcefully, despite not raising his voice. Imara knew what he was talking about and became nervous.

"I swear, I wasn't. I fought you with the power that I knew that I had, and all the skill that I had at the time." Vituo could see Imara was speaking the truth, but he just couldn't believe she was so easily beaten the time he had fought her and who he believed had been an imposter of her father. Kalin, however, was more concerned about another part of Oogtar's statement.

"So, Qilin has joined the Mujin Dynasty? He's . . ." Kalin's words caught in his throat; his feelings conspicuously made themselves known at this moment. But he cleared his throat and swallowed his sadness. "He's fallen that low?" The Hesura Prince's hard tone would have convinced anyone else, but now that his sadness was heard it could not be unheard by all present. Oogtar looked to the Nderu siblings, who all solemnly nodded for him to continue.

"Listen up, kids, cause this is gonna be a long story. I'll try to be brief, though." Oogtar tried, but even his sense of humor failed him as he took a breath.

"Qilin hasn't joined the Mujin Dynasty. Matter of fact, Syn hasn't even joined the Chimera Clan. Just like R-Corporation over in Europe, the 0th Secret Operations in America, and the Oceanbound Insurgency underwater, the Mujin Dynasty, and the Chimera Clan are in an equal alliance. With one Warwick Goodvibe," Oogtar explained. It was clear that nobody present besides Lugo had ever heard this name before, and it would be the Subterranean King who'd voice this.

"Who . . . who is he?" King Abdul asked, to which Oogtar's eyes seem to light with real anger. His tone remained the same, however.

"The man ultimately responsible for why all of the named factions are so well-supplied, well-organized and just generally as powerful as they are. The man who is only too happy to see the Elven Territories and the Kingdoms of Paradise at each other throats. And the man who was only too happy to see Emperor Mujin-Anmin's failures."

Zume and Auri both cringed in unison with King Abdul as they read his mind and saw the memory of the day Malkia's husband actually uttered the racial slur 'Dwarve' to the Subterranean King with no sense of irony in sight; he did this on live international television, at that.

"What do you propose?" Vituo finally asked the million-dollar question.

11:00 PM that Night:
Imara's Bedroom

Imara was finding it very difficult to sleep; her very first State of the Territories Conference was a momentous one indeed. Not only because of the plan Oogtar and the Changelings devised, but also because of what she was to do in two months' time. Imara never thought she'd be considered for the highest honor, and most daunting task, of participating in the Master Challenge. In fact, she found her father's words ringing in her head, despite what Oogtar had said concerning her talent.

"If I was worthy, why would my own father hate me so much? Why couldn't he see my talent?" Imara regretted, as she thought of all the ways she could have helped her father succeed. Tears fell from her eyes as she tried to put the thought of her deceased father out of her mind, as she drifted off to a turmoiled sleep.

Eight Years Ago

"MUJIN!" Imara found herself jarred awake by the sound of her father's enraged scream. She recognized it; it was the day her father attempted to storm the Imperial Palace. However, she remembered following Atto's suggestion and leaving the battlefield right about here; in fact, she watched her father look at her younger self retreating. Raj scoffed in disgust, and Imara's heart ached at the origin of Raj's disappointment in her.

However, Imara knew why her present self was not allowed to leave. She didn't want to watch, but she was forced to as Raj and his best friend Atto confronted an entire division of the Imperial Special Forces. Standing at the entrance promontory of the Imperial Palace was none other than Empress Malkia and her husband, the infamous Emperor Kato Mujin-Anmin.

The royal couple looked almost as worried as the elites that separated the two lone warriors, if not more. Imara knew what was coming; she almost wanted to tell the troops to simply cut their losses and run while they still could. Kato Mujin-Anmin was an Emperor that simply did not deserve the sacrifices that these good servicepeople were about to make.

Imara couldn't look away as one, then two more, than ten more, and then hundreds more gave shouts of battle and adrenaline as they ran toward Raj and Atto. With a smirk Raj activated his chi, then began to trot leisurely to the warriors sprinting at him with bad intent.

These brave men and women were sprinting to their deaths, as Raj powered through the first hundred troops like a heavy bowling ball through the lightest of pins. Raj needed no weapon as he handled and maneuvered through the onslaught with the greatest of ease. He need not throw more than one strike per opponent; at times he merely crippled a limb he caught as opposed to delivering a deathblow. Raj perhaps pulled some punches to entertain himself, and some of the luckier victims were simply disarmed and then thrown as harmlessly as possible in hopes that he could get as much sport as possible. Imara felt the hopelessness of the situation sink in; her father's Spectral power placed him on same level as that of the Slayer of Ten Thousand's, and unfortunately there was only two thousand troops guarding the Capitol.

Her heart sank even more when she noticed five priests conjure up two Thralls each with Impure Resurrection; she wanted to warn them to run, but once again her tongue wouldn't work as Raj's eyes lit with real anger at seeing the hated technique he could never master on his own.

But the keywords were "on his own." He had absolutely no problem overriding the control of the summoners if he could just make physical contact with the Thralls. With one tap on the head each, Raj seized control of all ten Thralls; they were now his as he used them to continue tearing through the Empress's elite forces. The five priests realized their mistake, and Raj for the first time used a weapon during his two-man coup by taking some swords from the fallen. The poor Sanctorum elites wasted precious time trying to dispel the Thralls when they should have conjured up barriers to stop Raj from launching his acquired swords through their faces.

Even though Raj equally divided his Spectral power eleven ways, he and his newly acquired undead servants still held the advantage over the remaining one thousand troops before him. At one point a Hayflick Dragon was summoned, but almost as soon as it was summoned and set upon Raj did he take advantage of an opening and cave its head in with a solid punch. Incredulously, the Hayflick Dragon did not rise ever again, and in fact dissipated once it had fallen to the ground, dead.

Imara had almost forgotten that Atto had chosen to simply support his best friend from a range, until she saw ten helicopters full of troops just above the battlefield. Big mistake giving Atto decent sized targets, for he gathered Nuclear chi in his right hand and Spatial chi in the other and fired them in a wave-motion fashion.

The reinforcement choppers all exploded, one after the other, as Raj and his stolen Thralls continued to fight through a thousand remaining troops. No, this wasn't a fight; this was a culling of a herd of lambs, with Raj as the evil wolf hunting more for sadistic sport than anything else.

Nowhere was this more evident than when Raj allowed one particularly brave spear woman to throw a few slashes, stabs, and kicks at him. Raj didn't dodge her attacks so much as he leaned out of range of her kicks or slumped out of the line of attack from her slashes and stabs. He eventually lost interest and snapped her spear in half with a well-timed punch. With the same hand that he broke her spear, Raj grabbed the hapless young woman by the throat. She squirmed, her feet kicking ineffectively as she was lifted off the ground.

"Having a woman defend his majesty? I thought he was more of a man," Raj taunted. Imara saw the look on Emperor Mujin-Anmin's face; she wondered if he was able to hear Raj from his vantage point. In any case, it would be the two remaining priests who seized the opportunity to blast Raj away and save his next victims' life. The energy beam that crashed into Raj did little more than shunt him away from the remaining troops, but it allowed the distance the two priests needed in order to gather precious energies and prompt the rest of the troops to join in the mass energy beam attack.

"Ah, so you want to start using firepower, then?" Raj said with a smirk. "Atto, out of the way," Raj said, and his best friend descended to ground level, landing behind the rebelling general. And when Atto did, Raj took a deep breath, gathering up some of his chi into his mouth. Right as the priests and the remaining troops unleashed their seven-Conversion combination attack, Raj bellowed out a Spirit Cannon. For just a moment, the beams clashed and stalemated.

But the keywords once again were "for just a moment." Soon, Raj's overwhelming Spectral chi brute forced its way past the more skilled, yet weaker chi of his opponents.

The cloud of dust kicked up required Imara to use the Sight of Oracles to continue observing the carnage, meaning some of the lesser troops were unable to see Raj burst through the cloud of dust to continue splitting skulls with his bare fists alone. Raj seemed uninhibited by the obscuring particles, as he continued laying into the remaining eight hundred troops. At one point, one of the priests attempted an Illusion. It was likely a Paralysis Hallucination, because that was what happened to the hapless priest as soon as Raj reversed it.

The look on his face as his own Illusion was turned back on him in a fraction of a second was the look this man died with as Raj seized the opportunity to literally kick this man's chin and lower jaw off his face. If any of the remaining troops hoped to distract Raj by going after the less combat-savvy Atto, this was quickly dashed by the ten stolen Thralls defending Raj's advisor with their undeaths.

Finally, Raj and Atto made it to the Imperial Palace. "COME OUT, YOU DAMNED COWARD!" Raj said as he blasted the palace door down. Imara's eyes teared up as she saw the younger Azuro and Chagua cower behind their mother. She recognized the teenaged Synturo, who swallowed his fear to step protectively in front of his mother and younger siblings, summoning up some Nuclear chi in one hand and Temporal chi in the other. Even Emperor Kato seemed to falter a bit at the look of murder in Raj's eye. He began to laugh in sadistic optimism as he stalked threateningly toward them.

Imara didn't want to watch this moment. The moment her father lost everything, including the power he once had. The moment Lugato Nderu, the Slayer of Ten Thousand, had teleported to the Imperial Family's rescue, alongside the Grand Priest. The moment she'd have told Raj and Atto to retreat while they still had all of their power. And most of all, the moment she'd have told them not to underestimate the teenaged Lugo before them.

As the world flashed white, indicating the end of the dream, Imara was just happy that the torturous memory was over.

10:30 AM
the Present Day

"So? Who's it gonna be? Come on, you got to tell us," the members of the Gimura Force begged their leader as soon as they had a break during training. They suspected that it was between Sol and Ron, but they all just had to ask. Imara giggled.

"I honestly haven't decided yet. But my partner for the Master Challenge needs to be someone I can trust my life with, so there's that," she said. One would be forgiven for thinking Imara was the Empress right now; she perhaps commanded more respect and admiration from the former outlaws than Malkia could ever hope to. "Adam, Jericho, and Hassan have all mentioned that they would rather continue to lead the Force in my absence, so they're ruled out. Sol and Ron, though . . ."

The murmurs sent through the gathered warriors conveyed disappointment and expectation at the same time. "Of course. Those two always were closest to her . . ." one said, clearly wishing it were him instead.

"Raj and Atto were inseparable. Of course, Ron was always going to have a leg up on little old us . . ." another lamented. Imara giggled; she honestly wondered if saving these men from a life of poverty and loneliness really was worth the unconditional adoration they were giving her.

"Not to mention Sol was usually the first one on the scene when Imara needed help," another posited, and Imara remembered how often Sol ran to her rescue. Imara wished she could bring both of them with her to tackle the Master Challenge

But Imara knew who needed it the most. Imara knew who she most trusted, even between Sol and Ron. It was the first man outside of her family she ever got acquainted with, who stuck by her even when there was no visible reward or even a "thank you" in it for him.

2:00 PM:

The Imperial Palace, Meditation Garden

"**W**ow . . . I . . . I honestly don't know what to say . . ." Ron said as he beheld the Jewel Shard he was given; the rainbow-colored shard that he and Imara would need to present to be admitted into the Master Challenge.

"You really shouldn't be surprised," Imara said. The rest of the Gimura Force simply bowed in respect to Imara's decision, though Sol noticeably looked almost disappointed by this. "After careful consideration, I've trusted you the most. Sometimes more than I trusted even my own brothers. Especially with certain secrets . . ." Imara's face turned red at that last part as she looked away. She had hoped it wasn't an open secret at this point.

"I'm pretty sure you've been trusting more than just me with said secrets," Ron said with a chuckle, as Imara blinked. The rest of the Gimura Force, especially Sol and those closest to Imara's age, silently concurred.

"What secrets?" Hassan asked, the boy truly and genuinely lost despite the looks from Adam and Jericho.

"Use your imagination, Hassan," Penelope said, chuckling at her own memories of her wild and sensual youth before she married Raj. Adam and Jericho both grimaced at their mother's words.

"We try not to, Mom," Jericho said. "Dad would have been better off if he didn't as well." The mood soured as soon as Raj was mentioned, especially among the younger men as they remembered Raj's reaction to the suggestion that Imara was fraternizing with the troops. This memory also shined a light on the fact that only Ron could have gotten away with turning on Imara's father as he did, and even then, perhaps Imara didn't hold it against him only because of the cavalier attitude Raj beheld his best friend's sacrifice with. Even so, Imara's sadness at her father's death was still visible.

"Raj was never the true leader of his own Force, nor was he even the reason his own household was in order. The sooner you realize that the better you'll feel about what happened to him. And the sooner you'll realize why the Empress and especially Prince Azuro place as much faith in you as they do," Ron reassured as he handed the Jewel Shard back to Imara.

"Well said, Jotomatu," Empress Malkia's voice sounded, and everyone bowed the minute they turned and saw the Elven Empress. To her right stood Azuro, King Oogtar, and King Abdul; and to her left stood the Grand Priest, then Lugo, then Zume and Auri. All of them concurred with the Empress, who continued to speak for them.

"We have no doubt that you will win the Master Challenge, and just as soon as you stop doubting yourself will you realize that you were destined for greatness from the very start. The fact that you can wield the Troll Scimitar alone is proof enough of that. But simply look behind you if you need more convincing," Malkia said as she pointed behind the next Grand Priestess.

Imara for the first time saw what many others saw. The entire Gimura Force, made up of those most societies would deem unscrupulous or lost causes, looked upon her with the utmost respect and adoration. She could command them all to commit suicide, and they'd scramble over who could do it the quickest. It occurred to her that almost all of these men would never have submitted to any other authority if not hers. She truly was the real power in the Gimura Force.

"You truly believe in me? You all truly believe that I can complete the Master Challenge?" Imara asked, to which Lugo spoke up.

"We believe you do not even need a partner to do so, in fact. However, with Ron at your side, you carry with you the entire morale and support of the Gimura Force. You will prevail, if for no other reasons than there is no challenge on Master Sheng's Island that can stop you once you recognize your abilities," Lugo said. Imara's eyes glowed, a smile tugging at her lips at seeing the concurrence of all those who believed in her, even where she didn't believe in herself.

"For all of you. I shall ace the Master Challenge."

The Next Day:
Goodvibe Syndicate Meeting Room

"So, that's what we're reduced to?!" Goodvibe screamed out, his voice carrying and echoing throughout the chamber. The other members of the Syndicate flinched at his roar of anger, but pointedly Qilin, Synturo, and Torune stood their ground. "Enough Spectral chi to overpower ten Soul Reapers, and you can't even ensure a goddamned Illusion is cast properly?!" Goodvibe bellowed out to Qilin. The Grandmaster of the Chimera Clan was unfazed.

"The Masai Five happened to show up at the worst possible time. You of all people should know that we can't always plan for blind fate and dumb luck," Qilin responded, striking a nerve as he reminded Goodvibe of a certain failure in the past.

"And you . . ." Goodvibe moved to who he'd hope would be a safer target in Synturo. "Your plan was worse than a failure. Because of your plan Oogtar and his Amphibians are no longer loyal to us AND the Kingdoms of Paradise, the Elven Territories, and its two subordinate monarchs called a temporary truce to their wars. Worse? You didn't even bring Grendella's yummy little niece back here!" The uncomfortable looks from the rest of the criminal underworld leaders at that last part was practically tangible. Even Qilin and Synturo visibly faltered at hearing these words.

Only two people present seemed able to hear that with no reaction. And one of them spoke up at this moment. "What's with all this sneaking around, anyway?" All eyes went right to the newest member of the Mujin Dynasty as soon as he spoke up. Torune didn't quite get that Goodvibe counted this as speaking out of turn, or simply overestimated the petulant billionaire's patience.

"Oh? You have a better idea?" Goodvibe required rhetorically. And Torune answered sincerely.

"Well, Imara and one of her boy toys are going to be doing the Master Challenge in a month. It's a simple matter of just ambushing the proceedings and taking her while she's alone. And this time, there won't be any distractions and wrenches in the plan," Torune said this as assuredly as if it would actually be that easy. Goodvibe seemed to glare for a moment, before he seemed to relent. In fact, he smiled at the idea metastasizing in his brain.

"Hmm . . . That's such a simple plan. So simple, it can't be botched or mishandled," Goodvibe said, becoming more and more optimistic as he spoke.

"But . . . Goodvibe . . ." Synturo started, in disbelief that his benefactor was even entertaining such a bold and direct scheme.

"So far, I have operated mostly in the shadows and through proxies and patsies such as all of you." Goodvibe wasn't even pretending that he respected anyone gathered at his table. C.G. Ristar and Qilin blinked at this; Goodvibe might have overestimated exactly what he could and could not say to his subordinate leaders just a bit.

"You do so because the last time you made a direct attempt to act on your plans, you were beaten, lost your first Syndicate and had to steal from the Rothchild Clan just to recoup the losses you incurred." Synturo didn't raise his voice, but his words drowned out every single other sound in the world right about now. Goodvibe glowered at Synturo and summoned his five swords in a formation around Synturo.

"Do not forget that I have lost the entire U.S. debt twice over and still have more resources and money than any of you could ever hope to see in your lifetimes," Synturo was unfazed; in fact, he seemed to be almost daring Goodvibe into acting on his threat.

"And do not forget why you failed the last time, Warwick," Synturo retorted, still just as calmly.

That this was coming from the much younger man, a man that was only barely older than his grandchildren, galled the multibillionaire beyond words. However, he then turned to Torune, who immediately felt an unfamiliar feeling of fear when their eyes met. "You!" Goodvibe said, his voice slamming into Torune's ears. In any other situation, Torune would have taken offense to an old man speaking so freely and rudely at him. But the floating swords that he found pointed at his jugular were a major factor in why he didn't.

"You, Synturo, and Qilin failed to bring me Maharajan Gimura's daughter using Synturo's plan. However, if you fail to execute my plan . . ." Torune blinked. He knew Goodvibe was seizing credit for the simple, yet effective plan, but could do nothing about it at this moment. The swords edged closer to Torune's throat as Goodvibe said this.

"AND WHAT IF THE PLAN NEVER GETS A CHANCE TO BEGIN? WILL THE YOUNG MUJIN BE HELD RESPONSIBLE FOR THAT WHICH IS BEYOND HIM?"

A sagely, wizened, yet only too powerful voice sounded. The gasps of shock and horror reverberated through the insulated meeting room. Everyone stood up and even Qilin, Synturo, and C.G. Ristar jumped in fright and took defensive stances at hearing this particular voice.

But the one most spooked was Goodvibe himself. "What?!" he exclaimed, withdrawing his swords and having them surround himself in a defensive formation. Goodvibe seemed as though he had seen and heard Satan himself. "SHOW YOURSELF!" Goodvibe barked out madly. The old multibillionaire sounded truly afraid. Any and all malice or disunity among the Goodvibe Syndicate was immediately forgotten. Whether they reported to R-Corporation, the Oceanbound Insurgency, the Chimera Clan, or the Mujin Dynasty made absolutely no difference right now as all of them stood in one accord against the unseen intruder.

"IF YOU WISH TO SEE, YOU MUST ALLOW ME TO BE SEEN," the disembodied voice said. No one except Goodvibe could comprehend the meaning of those words. He took a breath and calmed his nerves. He closed his eyes, and as soon as his chi was no longer riled up from being spooked, Goodvibe opened his eyes to see one of his erstwhile enemies appear. Right in the middle of what was supposed to be a top-secret installation.

"Huang Sheng . . ." Goodvibe said angrily at the old Chinese man standing in front of him. If you ever needed to see the personification of the "old, cryptic, mysterious master," here he was in the form of Master Huang Sheng. His luxurious white beard extended to his chest, which more than made up for the fact that he was otherwise bald. He was shorter than Goodvibe even when the petulant billionaire was hunched over, yet the fact that this thin, frail-looking senior citizen with a walking cane intimidated all present spoke volumes to how dangerous he could be.

"It is good to see you again, Warwick." When not projecting his voice using his chi, Huang Sheng even sounded like a wise, polite, and soft-spoken master of all combat styles. Goodvibe seethed; all except three took a step back when Sheng glanced in their direction. The old master was outnumbered more than forty to one, yet not a single person there had any illusion as to who was the one in danger should he choose to fight.

"How?! How could you possibly have found this hideout?!" Goodvibe asked incredulously.

"Warwick, there are no such things as secrets. Merely that which has been sought, and that which has not been," Master Sheng stated simply. He turned his back on Goodvibe, as he surveyed the gathered Syndicate members. His eyes settled on Torune.

"H-Hey, what . . . what do you want, old man?" Torune asked nervously, his legs shaking as he spoke. Goodvibe was about the only one brave enough to attempt to attack Master Sheng while his back was turned. All five of Goodvibe's floating swords careened toward the old master almost faster than even the trained eye could perceive.

But they'd never meet their target. In fact, the swords simply stopped in mid-air, without any visible input from Master Sheng. The keyword was "visible," however, for all present felt his chi activate and completely eclipse Goodvibe's. The swords were then teleported away; Goodvibe couldn't summon them back.

"Forty-five years later, and you are still predictable," Master Sheng said without even turning to face the flabbergasted Goodvibe.

"What is this, Sheng?! You think you can just walk in here and do as you please?!" Goodvibe barked out.

"My belief is not incorrect, as you are very aware. Settle your anger, Warwick. It will do nothing for you on this day, as it did nothing for you or your allies forty-five years ago," Master Sheng coolly replied.

Synturo found his words at this moment. "Calm down, Goodvibe. Let us hear what Master Sheng has to say." Goodvibe hesitated, before taking a step back. Master Sheng looked in Torune's direction.

"You and Chagua have much to discuss before the Master Challenge begins. You will go to her now," Master Sheng more commanded than said, and as soon as he was done speaking he pointed at Torune.

"Wha—?" Torune attempted, but he was teleported away in the blink of an eye.

"What's the meaning of this?!" Synturo asked, finally raising his voice and betraying his panic. Master Sheng did not turn to face the leader of the Mujin Dynasty.

"Do not worry about your sister or your cousin. Chagua required a Jewel Shard to be considered, and she obtained one six months ago. She requires a partner to officially participate in my Challenge, and now she has one." Synturo and Qilin seemed to follow. As did Goodvibe, and this was what influenced his next words.

"You talk about me not changing in forty-five years, yet here you are still continuing an outdated practice. Why not just re-summon your friends if you miss them that much?" Master Sheng simply narrowed his eyes at Goodvibe's words. The gap in power had only widened over the years, but Goodvibe perceived that this was about the only way he could hope to hurt the old master. And he was going to twist the knife as much as he could, for as long as he could.

"The four friends you speak of faced death with the knowledge that they shall ascend beyond anything we mortals are capable of. They are content with their places in the afterlife. But what about any of you? Which one of you present can say that you would find solace in your place in the afterlife?" Master Sheng said, though the fire under his tone told all present that Goodvibe likely struck a nerve. Right now was not the time to test the old master's patience.

"You've got what you've come for, I presume," Goodvibe said as powerfully as he could. He was half right; the other half of Master Sheng's reason for being here now came to the forefront.

"Warwick Goodvibe, forty-five years ago you attempted to strike a deal with the very same Neo-Spacian Empress you still treat with today. Aside from you and I, the only one present who remembers the original Syndicate . . ." Master Sheng pointed in the direction of the Oceanbound Insurgency's representatives. Specifically, he directed his attention to the leader of said Oceanbound Insurgency. ". . . Will understand why I tell you to quit now while you still have the opportunity." Master Sheng paused, as he looked directly to the kraken that led the Oceanbound Insurgency. The sadness in the old master's eyes betrayed his pity of the dethroned king, but he quickly hardened his visage once again

"You two witnessed the power of the Neo-Spacian Empres firsthand. Even with King Pintar's power, you could not hope to star against her. Even after the release of the Orc Emperor and the f Troll Vassals from their accursed armaments, the Neo-Spac escaped with her life and most of her power. There is not one p present who could have matched Pintar's power, nor the po any one of the Troll Vassals, let alone all of the aforementio once." Master Sheng looked to Goodvibe.

"But the next Grand Priestess, however, was able to m power of the strongest of the Troll Vassals without truly knov she's capable of. Besides your more . . . prurient goals . Sheng's disgust at Goodvibe's lecherous motives was visible, though Synturo suspected that it wasn't just the c this comment was directed toward. ". . . I am aware ' infinite well of untapped power is what you seek to ga' the most. With it, perhaps you could safely betray th Empress. If you were to get the next Grand Priestess '

groom her accordingly." Goodvibe involuntarily blanched at just how right Master Sheng was.

"Consider this my final warning, and my final imploration. I do not wish for my Challenge to be interrupted. However, if my wish is untenable, my wrath will be swift and unrelenting."

With that, the old master teleported, slowly fading away.

THE END.